"Pipe's a phallic symbol, you know," Sam said

"Is not," Hope said at once.

"Is, too." He nodded. "All these years you've been working at Palmer Pipe you've been substituting pipe for penises."

She half rose, reached behind her and grabbed up a pillow. "I have not!" She raised the pillow over her head.

"Hey, don't yell at me. I'm not the one with pipe envy." Sam rolled smoothly off the bed just as she slammed the pillow into the spot where he'd been lying.

At the doorway to the bathroom, in all his naked masculine glory, not at all shy the morning after, he turned to give her a wicked smile. "Don't move," he said. "I'm going to brush my teeth and get fresh supplies, and then I'm coming back to relieve your need for pipe. Forever."

Barbara Daly lives and writes in New York City. She loves it most of all during the holiday season, when the lights, the department store windows and the first snow of winter falling on the shoppers as they struggle down the crowded streets add to the festive feeling. What better setting for a love story?

She is a newcomer to feng shui, but is rapidly putting mirrors in strategic places and flutes on the beams and is convinced it's going to change the life she shares with her husband and Cairn terrier.

She once had a cat like the one in this book—and suspects she might not live through a second one.

A Long Hot Christmas is just the first of three books featuring the Sumner sisters. Don't miss Barbara's special Duets #69, *You Call This Romance!?* and *Are you for Real?*, coming to bookstores in February.

Books by Barbara Daly

HARLEQUIN DUETS
13—GREAT GENES!
34—NEVER SAY NEVER!

A LONG HOT CHRISTMAS
Barbara Daly

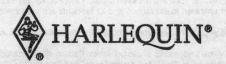

HARLEQUIN®

TORONTO • NEW YORK • LONDON
AMSTERDAM • PARIS • SYDNEY • HAMBURG
STOCKHOLM • ATHENS • TOKYO • MILAN • MADRID
PRAGUE • WARSAW • BUDAPEST • AUCKLAND

For Helen Daly, my mother-in-law,
best friend and lifelong card partner. I love you for loaning me
your son—and for letting me win once in a while.

Special thanks to:

Bonnie Tucker for getting me unstuck, Rob Clark for telling me
everything I've ever wanted to know about pipe, Kathleen Furey and
Patricia Garbutt for steering me toward the delights of feng shui and
to Susan Sheppard, who brings out the best in me.

ISBN 0-373-25959-X

A LONG HOT CHRISTMAS

Copyright © 2001 by Barbara Daly.

Visit us at www.eHarlequin.com

Printed in U.S.A.

1

HOPE SUMNER'S sisters were ganging up on her again.

"I was thinking a cat," she informed them. "I do not need a man."

"Just to go places with," Faith said.

"An escort, nothing more than that," Charity said.

"Because the holidays are coming up," Faith added.

Hope rued the day she'd taught them to make a conference call. With Faith in Los Angeles and Charity in Chicago, for a time they'd had no choice but to attack her separately. One-on-one, she was invincible. Against the two of them, she had to fight for her life. Or in this case, her lifestyle.

And what was wrong with her lifestyle? Nothing. She loved living in New York. She was a successful career woman who could afford elegant clothes, when she managed to find time to shop, luxurious vacations, if she ever found time to take a vacation, and an apartment with a fabulous view—where she rarely was, nor was she at the moment.

"Lana says he's a very nice man," Faith persisted.

"Lana? The punk-rock movie star? Lana dates leather jackets on motorcycles. You told me so yourself."

"That's how she met him," Faith said as though this made everything clear. "Her latest leather jacket is actually a software genius. The Shark defended him against *the big* software company."

"The Shark?"

"His real name's Sam Sharkey," Charity supplied helpfully. "They just call him The Shark."

"Oh. Did he win?"

"Well, of course," Faith went on. "And while they waited for the judge's decision, they got to talking, and Shark said he was sick of being the 'available bachelor' on everybody's list, but he's nowhere even *close* to wanting to get married, not until he makes partner at his law firm."

"Anyway," Charity interrupted, "Lana's leather jacket told Lana and Lana said, 'He sounds like Faith's sister Hope, and she's in New York, and The Shark's in New York,' and one thing led to another."

That's how bad it was. Her own sisters were shopping her around to lawyers who represented leather jackets accused of software plagiarism. The cat was sounding better every minute. A calico with pretty markings. Or maybe something with long, soft hair she could run her fingers through.

She liked her life. She loved her work. All she wanted was to be the first female, and at twenty-eight, the youngest person, ever to make vice president at Palmer. Then she'd be ready to enter the next phase of her life, which would include love and happiness, a man with thick, silky hair she could run her fingers through...

She'd been quiet too long. They might assume she was thinking it over, which she certainly wasn't. "Hey," she said in a "let's negotiate" tone, "I really appreciate what you're trying to do for me, but a man to take to parties isn't what I need to get me out of this little slump I'm in."

Her gaze darted to her monitor. She swiftly dragged a black seven onto a red eight, smiling when the elusive ace of diamonds appeared from beneath the seven. It was after nine at night. She was still at the office. She'd come to a stopping place at eight, unable to move forward effectively without input from colleagues who'd already left.

Even her nemesis, whom she privately referred to as St. Paul the Perfect, had gone home to his lovely wife and children. She knew he had, because he'd poked his head through the door to see if she was still there, and when he saw she was, had been forced to make up an elaborate excuse for his early departure. Some nonsense about rehearsal for the church pageant in which his tiny son had the lead role—Baby Jesus—and his daughter was head angel.

No reason for her not to go home, yet here she sat, playing solitaire.

She'd drag the ace later. "What I think," she went on, "is get a cat and cozy up the apartment a little bit. Sheila's sending me this decorator she says everybody's raving about. Her name's Yu Wing."

Tiny shrieks came at her from the receiver. "You're using a decorator *Sheila* recommended?" Charity squealed.

Being orphaned in early childhood had made Hope and her sisters unusually close. Even now, strung out from one coast to the other, they got together often, monitored each other's activities and knew each other's friends. Sometimes this was a good thing, sometimes not. "Yes a decorator *Sheila* recommended," Hope said, feeling defensive. "She uses *feng shui*. Sheila swears that she..."

"Sheila's insane," Faith declared.

"Lana isn't?"

There was a short silence before Charity said, "The last time I saw Lana I thought she'd matured considerably."

"Love has made all the difference," Faith said in her dreamy voice. Faith had always been a dreamer. She was thirty now, and Hope thought it was about time she found a man whose feet were firmly planted on this earth. Now *that* might make a difference.

"As it does for so many people," Charity said. Whatever Charity's tone indicated, it was not dreaminess. The youngest sister and the family beauty, she had a brain like a Pentium chip. She was twenty-six, and so far she hadn't found a man—lover *or* employer—who was able to see past her pretty face, although Hope could hardly blame the male population for that particular weakness.

"Just because love makes some people happy..."

"Who said anything about love?" Charity said.

"We're just talking about an arrangement," Faith said.

"To get you through the holidays," Charity said. "You have all those parties to go to and you hate going alone. I can hear it in your voice."

"Lana says he does, too," Faith said, "hates going alone, that is. Having women treat him as if he's up for grabs."

"So you and The Shark can go out together as protection for each other," Charity concluded in the voice of one who is confident she has built a solid argument.

"If you like him, of course," Faith said.

"Whether I like him wouldn't matter, would it, if we're just talking about an arrangement," Hope said unwisely.

"So you'll meet him? See if you two can make a deal?" The tiniest show of interest from Hope, and Faith moved in for the kill.

"*He* likes the idea." That was Charity, sneaking up from the rear.

"You already set it up?" Now that was going too far.

"Of course not. We just gave him your number."

"Numbers," Charity clarified. "Home, office, digital..."

"You told him I was interested?" Hope was already halfway out of her chair, grabbing for her coat and briefcase. To hell with the ace.

"Well, sort of," Faith admitted.

"She had to get the ball rolling," Charity said in her reasonable way. "We knew you wouldn't."

"I'm cutting you two out of my will!" Hope yelled.

"You have a will?" she heard Faith say before she hung up on them.

THE NEXT NIGHT, Wednesday night, Hope was home at seven. Usually, Thursday was the only night she came home at seven, but Sheila had made the appointment with the decorator, Yu Wing, for Thursday, forcing Hope to do her Thursday routine on Wednesday.

While she wouldn't admit it to Faith and Charity, she was pretty annoyed at Sheila for her highhanded behavior. It had disrupted her schedule and had gotten her Palm Pilot in a tizzy while she shuffled everything around.

But she was trying to be more flexible. Wasn't that what really worried her sisters, that she was sliding into a routine that was presently going to harden like concrete until she could never break free from it?

Good grooming, to Hope, was simply part of the image she had to maintain, that of a successful corporate woman. The "routine" she followed religiously on *Thursday* and Sunday evenings involved a quick dinner, after which she applied a masque to her face and gave her feet a good soak in a foot spa that vibrated. While invisible hands massaged her arches, she gave herself a manicure. When her fingernails were dry, she did a pedicure, and, at last, removed the hardened masque and with it, anything resembling dirt, toxins, flaking skin and incipient blackheads.

She shed her navy suit and navy silk shell and put on a white terrycloth robe. It felt good, warm and cozy, unlike the atmosphere of her apartment. Padding into the kitchen in matching terry slippers, she ran through her collection of TV dinners and selected Chicken Marsala with pasta and green beans, which she tossed into the microwave.

It had been a big decision whether the second grooming should be on Wednesday or on Thursday. Once she'd settled on Thursday, though, it had become a habit, and she intended to tell Sheila it was pretty darned unsettling to have to...

She suddenly felt more cross with herself than with Sheila. "Stop it," she said aloud to the sterile white-and-chrome kitchen, and the microwave answered with a "ping."

A MIRACLE HAPPENED to Samuel Sharkey that evening. The client he was scheduled to meet for drinks came down with a virus of the tree-felling variety and Sam found himself with a window in his schedule. He had a full hour and a half before he had to meet a group of clients for dinner, time enough to get a bothersome little detail out of the way.

He'd enjoyed defending Dan Murphy against the big company who alleged that Dan had lifted a program of theirs and gotten it on the market before they did. And he'd liked the cute, funny actress Dan was dating. Lana, that was her name. When Dan had started talking about Lana, it had somehow led Sam to tell Dan about *his* love life, which was a vacuum. It was Dan who'd come up with the—Sam couldn't help smiling as he searched through a stack of cards for the one with all the phone numbers on it—quirky, creative notion that The Shark needed another shark to swim with.

This woman was the perfect companion shark, Lana had promised him. Sam didn't believe it for a minute, but he was willing to go as far as to check it out for himself.

He found the card. He dialed the office number. When he got her voice mail—a cool, professional voice, he observed—he tried her digital phone. More voice mail, same cool voice. He glanced at his watch. Seventwenty. If she was already at home, she might not be the kind of woman he was looking for. Still, he had started it, he might as well finish it. He dialed.

HOPE ATE the Chicken Marsala without tasting it, which was probably all to the good.

Now the routine. Heavy-duty conditioner on the hair, wrap the hair up in a towel. Put on the masque. She spread the green paste on carefully. The label promised miracles, and expensive as it had been, it had better deliver. She was rinsing her hands when the phone rang.

"Hope Sumner?"

"Who's calling?"

"Sam Sharkey. Lana West got your number from Faith..."

"Oh, yes," said Hope. The lawyer, the one who had to make partner before he made a proposal. He was calling so soon? She hadn't really made up her mind yet, or actually she had. She'd decided to say no.

"I have a free hour or so I wasn't planning on. Wondered if I could come by and meet you. This is a pretty crazy idea, but I promised Dan I'd give you a call."

"Dan. The..."

"My client. The boy wonder of software."

"Oh." *Lana's leather jacket.* "Well, I agree it's a crazy idea," Hope said tightly. No other way she could say it. The masque was hardening rapidly. "Maybe we could just tell whatzisname we talked and decided against it."

"Actually," he said, "I've been thinking about it some."

"I guess I have, too," Hope said, "but I can't see you tonight. I'm wearing a masque."

Sam stopped himself just in time to keep from saying, "Hey, kinky." When his intelligence kicked in, he realized she wasn't talking a Little Bo Peep mask but that stuff women put on their faces—why, he didn't know. The masque explained the change in her voice. Now she sounded uptight.

"It has to stay on for forty-five minutes," she went on. "Otherwise, I might consider at least discussing an arrangement with you. Briefly."

So she *was* thinking about it. They must both be desperate. "Don't worry about how you look," he said. It was going to make *him* crazy if he couldn't fit this obligation into the free time that had dropped into his lap. "She already told me you were presentable."

"My *sister* described me as *'presentable'*?" The voice dripped ice.

Sam cursed himself. He was a lawyer. He was supposed to know how to choose his words, and if he couldn't choose the right ones, to keep his mouth shut. "No, I didn't talk to your sister. I asked Dan's girlfriend if you were presentable and she said sure. She said it in a positive way," he added for good measure. "Not like, 'sure she is.' More like 'she sure is!'" He winced just listening to himself. *Come on, Hope Sumner, say yes. We're wasting time.*

"We're wasting time."

Sam dropped his brand-new phone. Sweeping it up off the icy pavement, he heard Hope's, "Hello? Hello?"

"Sorry about that," he muttered.

"I was just saying, we might as well get this taken care of one way or the other."

"My thoughts exactly. I'll see you in—" He looked up at the number on the canopy that sheltered the entrance to a large, modern Westside apartment building "—a couple of minutes."

HOPE OPENED the door and peered out. What she wanted to do next was slam the door in his face and lean against it until her knees stopped trembling.

She'd been prepared for an attractive man. Good clothes and neat grooming had to be just as important in the legal world as they were in the corporate world, and this man had told Leather Dan right up front that he was aiming for the top. She'd expected him to be smart, well-educated and career-driven. What she was not prepared for was six two or three or four of bone and muscle, of shoulders and long legs, of sheer male power in a black overcoat. For short, thick dark hair, the kind of rich, deep tan she couldn't get even if she did throw skin health to the four winds and give it a try, and a pair of very blue eyes that examined her with thinly veiled curiosity.

It would be so, so wonderful if her face weren't green.

On second thought, she was grateful to have the masque to hide behind. His masculinity was overpowering. This was a man a woman could actually *want* to be with. And that wasn't the deal at all.

In fact, they didn't have a deal yet, and they weren't going to make a deal. A man like this could affect her attention span.

But she couldn't slam the door, and she couldn't take time to recover. "Sam?" she said briskly, hoping somehow he wouldn't be, that he was a totally different man who'd come to the wrong door. "Alias 'The Shark'?"

"That's me," he admitted.

With a strong feeling that she was doing the wrong thing, she opened the door wider and waved him in. "I'm sorry about the mudpack," she said. "If I'd known..."

"No problem," Sam said, shrugging out of his overcoat and revealing a dark pinstriped suit. "I've got sisters. I've seen them with green faces and cucumbers on their eyes."

He smiled. His smile wasn't anything like the calculating curve of a shark's grin. It was warm and compelling. It sent out powerful vibes, although she had a feeling he had no idea his testosterone had sprung a potentially explosive leak. Hope's knees buckled again, but she locked them in place and said, "I'll take your coat. Please sit down. Would you like a glass of wine? I'm afraid I can't join you, because I still have..."

"No, thanks," he said simultaneously. "I still have..."

"...work to do," they finished together, and Hope couldn't resist the temptation to smile back at him. Feeling her face crack sobered her up at once, but it didn't slow down her pulse rate, still the pounding of her heart or lessen her sudden awareness that under the sexless terrycloth robe she was wearing—nothing.

She didn't need her Palm Pilot to tell her it was time, definitely time, to pull herself together and direct her thoughts to a higher plane.

"That's our problem." She let out a rounded sigh that settled the masque back into place. "At least my sisters think it's a problem."

"Liking your work?" Sam The Shark took a look around the room. "Great view," he murmured. Then he aimed himself half-heartedly at one of her plump, velvety armchairs, seemed to give up on that goal, glanced at her deeply cushioned taupe sofa and finally slid onto it, carefully bypassing the knife-sharp corners of her smart glass coffee table.

"Loving it," Hope said. She couldn't help noticing that he didn't look any more comfortable on the expensive Italian design statement than she felt. She'd paid extra to have it stuffed with down. How much more comfortable could you get?

She made a mental note to ask the interior designer what the problem might be. For the first time, she thought she actually needed a decorator.

If she wasn't careful, she'd start thinking she needed

a man. Noticing that she was still milling around her own living room, she took the armchair that sat at a right angle to Sam Sharkey. That way she could get another look at his profile, his long, elegant nose and his to-die-for lashes.

"I don't even know if I love my work," Sam said, looking thoughtful. "I don't have time to think about it. All I know is that I'm determined to succeed at it."

"Well. Me, too," said Hope. The words "vice president" lit up in her mind like a Times Square theater marquee. She gave Sam a closer look, wondering if "partner" had just lit up for him.

"Tell me about your job," he said, and turned the full force of his riveting dark-blue gaze on her.

The "vice president" sign faded as another, quite disturbing message lit up inside her. The impact was powerful enough that she had to dig deep for the name of her company, but it finally surfaced. "I'm at Palmer. In Marketing."

"Palmer. It rings a bell. I should know what Palmer does, but..."

She'd just drifted into a vision of Sam parting her robe to move his hands sinuously across her breasts when it all came back to her, her job, her true love, the real object of her deepest desire.

"Pipe," she said.

SHE SAID the word the way another woman might say *pearls* or *Pashmina*, *pâté* or *Porsche*. She all but licked her lips.

"Pipes? Meerschaums? Briars? Hookahs?"

"Pipe. Copper, plastic, cast iron, galvanized steel. Life flows through pipe. Pipe runs the world, and Palmer Pipe runs it better."

He gazed at her, feeling stunned. "Is that original with you? That 'Pipe runs the world' line?"

"Of course not," she said. "It came from the ad agency." She paused. "I picked the ad agency."

She looked at him so expectantly she reminded him all of a sudden of one of his sisters' kids wanting approval for a dive he'd just done or a basket he'd just made. And he did his best to make them feel good about each small victory.

He'd been lying about seeing his sisters in mudpacks and cucumbers. He'd seen them in curlers, no makeup and one of Dad's wornout shirts, but his sisters didn't have the time or the money to take care of themselves the way a woman like Hope did. They considered it a major victory to get their hair washed and their kids in shoes.

It was up to him to change all that, change their hand-to-mouth existences, turn them into upwardly mobile middle-class citizens, educate those kids—

He'd assigned his family a compartment in his mind that he visited when he needed to, but he never enjoyed the visits. Right now wasn't the time to go there.

"It's a good slogan," he said in an approving tone. If it had been one of his nephews, he'd have said, "You did good."

"Thank you. It's working. That's all that matters. And you? I mean, your work. I know you're a lawyer, but..."

"An associate at Brinkley Meyers."

"Brinkley Meyers? Your firm is representing Palmer in the Magnolia Heights case."

Sam snapped his fingers. "That's why it sounded familiar."

"Are you involved in the case?"

"Let's hope it doesn't come to that." He smiled. "I'm in litigation. My department won't get involved unless the case goes to court."

"Oh, it won't," she said with obvious confidence. "Now. You were saying you're an associate at Brinkley Meyers..."

She meant, "Let's get to the point." He leaned forward, meeting her green face head on to be sure she understood the seriousness of his situation. "A *single* associate. Who's determined to make partner. This year, preferably."

Something he said had gripped her attention. A pair of green eyes—really nice green eyes, he noted in passing—gave him their full attention. "So you're the 'fresh meat' at every party. You're the one they invite because they have a daughter, a friend, somebody they're sure they can match you up with. And you can't refuse, because you don't want to offend anybody who could influence your future."

"You've been there."

"I live there," she said, lowering her green face and balancing it on her fingertips. Thick, dark lashes fluttered down to brush the surface of the masque. "You just described my entire social life. I'm determined to make vice president for Marketing when August Everley retires in January, which means every move I make right now has a direct influence on my future."

He fell silent, taking a minute to wallow in self-pity and feeling that Hope was in there wallowing with him.

"If you don't show an interest it makes them mad," he went on when he felt they'd wallowed enough. "If you do show an interest and don't follow up on it, it makes them madder." He paused for a frustrated sigh.

"A person who doesn't understand, somebody like your sister Faith, let's say, wonders why you don't just find a real man friend and cut through all that nonsense."

Hope raised her head and visibly stiffened her backbone. "Or your sisters," she said. "They probably don't stop to think about the time it would take to find a woman you really enjoyed, time you don't have, and then the time that woman would demand from you once you'd found her."

"Time and commitment."

"Which neither of us is ready for."

"You got that right."

"What we're talking here is the possibility of a no-strings kind of escort arrangement. I go with you to your parties, you go with me to mine."

"We act friendly enough to make people think we're already spoken for."

"Right." Hope bit out the word and gazed at him with suddenly flashing eyes. "But let's get one thing straight. If we make this *ridiculous* arrangement, don't even think about calling me 'arm candy.'"

He struggled to keep his mouth from twitching, and when he'd gotten it straightened out, he narrowed his eyes. "Same thing goes for you," he said. "If we make this *extremely practical* arrangement, I'm not your 'arm candy' either."

IF HE'D FELT like expressing his true feelings, which he didn't, Sam had concluded that Hope Sumner would do fine. He liked the spunk she'd just shown. Without the green face she'd be attractive enough. One of those women who knew how to distract you from their flaws with expensive haircuts and makeup. She was well-spoken. She'd make a decent impression on Phil, the Executive Partner he reported to, and Angus Mc-Dougal, senior partner in Litigation, and she'd rear their children—one girl, one boy—with energy and intelligence.

But he was getting way, way ahead of himself. Five years ahead, maybe. The token girlfriend was for now, the suitable wife not until he'd made partner and collected a few years of percentages of the law firm's profits. Not until he felt invulnerable, professionally and financially.

The green eyes, spectacular green eyes, actually, gazed at him out of a matching face, and there seemed to be a lot of brown hair tucked under the institutional white towel. Brown hair, green eyes, average American coloring. You couldn't go wrong with that. She was a little taller than average—maybe five seven—but as tall as he was, that was fine. He couldn't tell what was tucked under the hotel-style white terry robe, except that the sash outlined a small waist and the robe hourglassed promisingly above and below it.

None of that mattered much. Just gravy. Yes, she'd do. Sam wished he could say so and get back to work, but unfortunately it was also necessary to convince her *he'd* do. Plus—he had one more question to ask her.

She blinked a couple of times, apparently adjusting to the idea that he didn't want to be arm candy either, and glanced openly at her watch. Sam took this as a good sign. "Well, Sam, it seems we're in agreement so far. Now that we've met each other, let's give the arrangement a little further thought before we touch base again."

Sensing that he might have passed muster, he relaxed, as much as he could in this room. It wasn't the sofa. The sofa was cushy. The apartment was cushy. Mentally he compared it with his own Spartan digs. Weird he'd feel more comfortable there. She wouldn't, though, and he'd never take her there, not even...

He tensed up again. "One more thing," he said. "How do you feel about sex?"

She froze. The word hung in the air like an especially acrid room deodorizer. Mesmerized, Sam watched a crack widen in the green masque, starting at the bridge of her nose and forking off to both temples. He suspected she'd tried to raise her eyebrows.

"I don't mean now," he assured her, "or even soon, not until we trust each other. But sex is one of the important things I don't have time for." Her steady unblinking stare was starting to make him nervous. "I mean time to develop a relationship to the point that..." He didn't get this rattled when a judge was staring him down in court. "I thought maybe you had the same problem, and we could include it in..." He halted. "Or maybe you don't..."

"Like sex?" she said. The crack deepened. "Want sex? Need sex? Of course I do, Sam. I'm a perfectly normal woman. But surely men have ways to... I mean, I know they... But of course, it's not the same as..."

It was her turn to be rattled. But only for a moment. The gleam suddenly returned to her eyes, and Sam had a feeling she was seeing a whole new market for pipe.

"Add it to your list of things to think about before we talk again," he said, regaining his calm.

"Shall we say early next week?"

Sam strode down the hall toward the elevator, bemused by the final question she tossed at him as they traded business cards. "Are you allergic to cats?" she'd asked him.

He wasn't, but he was curious to know why it mattered to her. His interest was short-lived. A few minutes later he had his laptop up and running in the bar of the restaurant where his clients would soon join him, doing the only thing he really felt comfortable doing. Work.

2

"Miss Yu Wing to see you."

"Send her up," Hope told the doorman. She checked out her apartment one more time. The magnificent view of Central Park and beyond it, the lights of the Upper East Side and the towers of midtown glittered through the huge plate-glass windows in both the living room and the bedroom. Bed made, aluminum foil from TV dinner in trash, pillows plumped, desk neat...she didn't know what an interior designer, even one of Yu Wing's reputation, could find to change.

The bell jangled, she flung the door open in a hospitable manner—and took in a quick, startled breath.

The small, thin woman who waited in the hallway had the biggest head of bleached-blond hair Hope had ever seen. The coat she carried appeared to have been made from a number of Afghan hounds. She fluttered a Stetson from one hand like a Victorian lady fluttering her hanky.

It was obvious why she was holding her hat. She'd never have gotten it on top of the hair. The ice-blue eyes that sparkled out at Hope from a narrow, sharp-featured, weatherbeaten face held a quick intelligence, though, that got Hope's attention.

A white Western-style shirt, faded blue jeans that stretched over her bony hips and high-heeled, tooled boots completed the picture.

The hallucination.

"Yu Wing?" Hope said. She didn't smile. She was poised to slam the door at any moment.

The woman breezed right past Hope into the living room. "Actually, sugah, the name's *E-w-i-n-g*, Maybelle Ewing, but folks expect a feng shui expert to have a kinda Asian name."

Hope glommed onto the one thing the woman had said that she understood. *"Feng shui?"* she asked in a high, thin voice. She cleared her throat. "You *are* the decorator."

"Sure am. A licensed interior designer and *feng shui* goo-roo."

Hope was translating Maybelle Ewing's deep Texas drawl into normal New York-speak as fast as her mind could function.

"Oh, my land!" Maybelle shrieked suddenly.

Of course. Ms. Ewing had noticed the view, the reason the small apartment was so expensive. All the chairs faced it. Her bed faced it. It didn't matter how you furnished an apartment when you had a view like this one.

Hope was so surprised she jolted backward when Maybelle's hand pressed against her forehead. The hand was dry and as bony as the rest of the woman. "You could make yourself sick in a place like this," Maybelle said in a hoarse whisper. She frowned. "You don't feel feverish. You been havin' any of them psychological problems?"

"No," Hope snapped. "Look, Yu Wing, I mean..."

"Just call me Maybelle."

"Look, Maybelle, all I want is to make this place a little cozier, make it look a little more lived-in."

"It will, hon, when you start living in it." Maybelle's

voice grew softer, lost its shrill quality. "I bet you hate coming home, am I right?"

Hope stared at her.

"Well, don't you worry about it no more, because Maybelle's going to fix everything."

How? Rope and tie it into submission? "Of course I would need an estimate from you before we enter into any sort of agreement," Hope said. Recalling one's purpose in engaging in a dialogue was a good way to keep from getting rattled. "Or perhaps you'd rather I gave you a budget."

"Whatever," Maybelle said with an airy wave of her hand. "We're not to that point yet. Let's see what I can do for a couple hundred dollars first. Mind if I take some pictures?"

"Yes," Hope said. The cool, serene African head on the stand in one corner had cost as much as she earned in a month. The huge bowl, a piece of glass art, was worth almost as much. Good investments, both of them. For all she knew, this insane woman was here to case the joint.

Maybelle wouldn't have a problem getting the bowl out, either. All she had to do was wear it over her hair. Then she could put the Stetson on the African head and...

"Please sit down," she invited Maybelle. Remembering one's manners—that was another good way to fight down rising hysteria. "May I get you a drink?"

"Sure," Maybelle said. "Some coffee'd be real tasty about now with bedtime coming up."

"Decaf?"

"Not if you've got the real stuff."

Hope headed for the kitchen to start a small pot of Hawaiian Kona, trying not to breathe the fumes in case they were enough to keep *her* awake. When she got back to the living room with Maybelle's cup of deadly insomnia in hand and a glass of sparkling water for herself, she found her new decorator circling the room.

Hope fell into step behind her. It was interesting the way they circled a while before they chose seats. Last night Sam Sharkey had done the same thing. The few times she'd entertained, her guests had done it, too, as though they were looking for a more comfortable spot from which to enjoy the view.

Just now, she was feeling a quite surprising need to make Sam comfortable. But not necessarily to enjoy the view. Something unfamiliar pinged inside her.

She quickly sat down, arbitrarily choosing one of the squishy taupe chenille armchairs and perching uneasily on its edge. Back to business. "Where exactly did you get your training?" she asked, narrowing her eyes.

"A correspondence course," said Maybelle. She deposited her cup on an end table. "Give me a hand with this, hon." She seemed intent on dragging the other armchair across the room where it faced the door with its back to the view.

Hope closed her eyes briefly, then hurried to help, just to save the floors. A correspondence course interior designer. Her sisters were right. Sheila was crazy, and if she ever saw her again, which she never intended to, she'd throttle her. "How did your interest in decorating come about," she said faintly, lowering her side of the chair to the floor. Thank goodness she hadn't signed anything yet.

"Well," the woman began when she'd settled into the chair, "first off, I was stuck down there in Texas on my husband's family ranch when he up and died."

"Oh, I'm sorry," Hope murmured.

"Don't be," Maybelle assured her. "It was him or the bull and the bull had a hell of a lot more character. Cuter, too, in his way." Her gaze grew thoughtful.

Hope's mouth formed an *O*. Her eyes sought out the phone on the end table beside her. How fast could she dial 9-1-1? She was already reaching for the receiver when the phone rang. She grabbed for it. Maybe the police were calling to warn her that a madwoman was on the loose.

"Hope? Sam."

"Sam?" Hearing from Sam wasn't on today's agenda. In fact, she'd assumed Sam would hear from her, not the other way around. That way she would have been prepared for the sound of his voice. This way, she hadn't been, and she was annoyed by the stab of heat, the sudden heaviness in the pit of her stomach. She locked her knees tightly together and sat up very straight. "We're scheduled to talk next week, I believe. I entered it in my Palm Pilot and synchronized it with my desktop calendar. The decorator is here now, so..."

"This'll just take a minute. It's an emergency."

He didn't sound as if he were dying, unaided, on a lightly traveled road. Hope drew her brows together. "What kind of emergency?"

She'd spent her hypothetical lunch hour—ten minutes eating yogurt and an apple at her desk—trying to imagine having sex with him as a purely therapeutic measure. "Have sex twice and call me in the morning if you're not better." And she'd decided—maybe. Or maybe not.

Out of the corner of one eye she watched Maybelle shaking her head and tsk-tsking. Meanwhile, Sam was delivering a staccato message into her left ear.

"The firm's executive partner is having a dinner

party tomorrow night. One of the guests met his Maker this afternoon. The partner's wife is deeply moved, but she's committed to the party. The problem is two empty spaces—the widow's not in a party mood—at a table set for sixteen at two-hundred-fifty dollars a plate." He paused. "Are you following me?"

"Closely," Hope said. "The caterer's going to charge for sixteen regardless. As a junior member of the firm you have to fill those two spaces."

"You're familiar with the system."

"Intimately." In fact, that was one of the reasons she might actually need Sam, or even better, somebody like him who didn't mention sex in their first meeting.

She had to admit she'd like it if this new man, the one who didn't mention sex in their first meeting, had a voice like Sam's. It was warm and deep, and it rolled over her like a soothing wave, although the way he sounded now was more like being in a stinging shower.

Maybelle wasn't in her chair any longer. Hope paced around with the phone until she sighted her in the bedroom, exploring the apartment uninvited and still tsk-tsking.

"Will you fill one of those spaces?"

"What? Oh." She refocused on Sam. "Is this important to you?" She'd read the books, gone to retreats, attended seminars at company expense, and she knew what questions to ask. She'd almost said, "Is this a step toward your goal?" but somewhere in her head she heard the echoes of her sisters' exasperated sighs.

"Real important. The boss's wife is after me."

"Your hostess tomorrow night?" She was pretty impressed with herself for following the conversation.

Maybelle was in the kitchen now, thumping the walls, looking for joists.

"So far she's only managed to signal me by wiggling her eyebrows and running her tongue over her lips. But those big Connecticut estates have pool houses, conservatories, butlers' pantries. Imagine what could happen if I said yes to her. Imagine what could happen if I said no to her."

"Screwed," Hope said. "Either way. You, I mean, not her. I mean..." She was glad he couldn't see her blush. Maybelle did, though, and gave Hope a knowing look before she trotted into the bathroom, brandishing a wrench.

"Will you come? Be my bodyguard?"

Hope could tell his problem was a serious one. So was hers. She had to get back to Maybelle before the woman started disassembling the plumbing. "Okay, I'll help you out. We'll call it a trial run."

"Pick you up tomorrow at five."

"Five o'clock? In the afternoon?" Even Maybelle faded from her mind. Hope did her best work after five.

"Lots of traffic on Friday. Long way to Connecticut. Party starts at seven. Can't be late."

She thought about it. "Okay, then. Pick me up at the office."

He was silent for a second. "It's black tie."

"No problem," said Hope.

"Five."

"The 48th Street entrance."

"I'll be there."

It was sort of a relief knowing she could delay coming home tomorrow. What was it with this apartment? What was it with Maybelle and all that tsk-tsking?

"Sorry for the interruption," she said, settling down again and feeling relieved when Maybelle followed suit. "Let's see, we'd gotten past the bull..."

"Yeah. Anyhoo," Maybelle said, picking up the thread without difficulty, "I got right bored that first winter after he was gone, what with nobody to fight with and only three channels on the television. But one morning I was watching this arithmetic program, Geometry, they call it—"

Hope's eyes widened.

"You know, one of them college courses they do on TV? Anyway, right after that they was advertising these University of Texas—" She pronounced it "Tegzis." "—correspondence courses and I sent off for the catalog. Whoo-ee, what a lot of junk you could learn without setting foot off the ranch!"

Hope felt her brain whirling in slow ellipses. Getting a little closer to Earth, then spinning way out into space. "So you sent off for a Geometry course."

"Calculus. I'd pretty much gotten the hang of Geometry and the catalog said take Calculus next."

"Oh."

"Then a course in lit-tra-chure."

"Contemporary American literature?"

"Nope, Mid-yeeval. You know, them sexy *Canterbury Tales*? Whoo-ee, they sure made me wish I had Hadley back for a long weekend. Then I said to myself, 'Girl, your hands are way more bored than your head.' And that was the truth, what with the ranch hands doing the outside work and their wives coming in to clean and cook. So I took a beautician course."

"A correspondence course in hairdressing?" The ellipse lengthened dramatically.

"Yeah. Well, that was a bust, with nobody but the

sheep to practice on. The ranch hands' wives wouldn't let me get anywhere close to them with my shears. But I can do my own hair real good," she said cheerfully. "Saved me many a penny, let me tell you."

"I can see that," Hope murmured. "How long did it take you to finish all those courses."

"Almost six months! Them courses was hard!" Maybelle's gaze shot over her shoulder, then flitted from one corner of the room to the other. "Honey," she said suddenly, "have you got an extry mirror I could hang over there on that wall?"

"Mirror? Well, no, all the mirrors are sort of attached to things, or doing their various..."

"No matter. I'll bring some by tomorrow." She frowned. "Don't want to wait long, though. Anyways, next thing I did was try my hand at making dishes and stuff. Old man Abernathy brung the kiln out to the ranch in his big truck and I did that until the ladies got to complaining about dusting all the new crockery. Then landscape design, but I couldn't get nuthin' much to grow out there in West Texas but cactus. This place sure could use some greenery," she added.

Hope wondered if Maybelle could be trying to hypnotize her. This was the most outrageous—at least the most different—face it, the most *interesting* conversation she'd had in ages. And she didn't have to say a word, just listen to Maybelle's chirping voice, which went so well with her chicken-like appearance. She could listen to Maybelle and think about Sam Sharkey. She was going out with Sam tomorrow night. No, not really going out with Sam, just accompanying Sam, protecting him from the boss's wife, but still...

"...feng shui," she heard Maybelle say.

Hope switched gears.

"And I said what the heck is that? So naturally I had to find out. And you know *what* I found out?" The question was clearly rhetorical, because Maybelle forged on. "If I'd known all that stuff before, Hadley and me might of got along a sight better."

"How." It wasn't a question, just a polite murmur. How could anybody get along with this idiot savant? Poor Hadley must have thought he'd died and gone to everlasting steam heat turned way up by the time the honeymoon was over. He'd apparently been desperate enough to engage in combat with a bull. Didn't that say something about the mood the man was in?

"That's what I'm going to show you, hon," Maybelle said with another of those abrupt softenings of her usual shrillness. She shot up out of the armchair, shouldered a brown leather purse that reminded Hope of a feedbag and got the Stetson twirling on one finger. "Can I have the run of the house for a coupla weeks?"

Absolutely not! Hope got up, too. "First I really do insist on having an—"

"—estimate. Budget." Maybelle sighed. "Honest to gosh, if you yuppies could get your minds off money for a split second…"

She was moving rapidly toward the door with Hope in her wake. "…and credentials," Hope said firmly. "Was the correspondence course the end of your professional training?"

Maybelle spun. "Lands no! I spent two years in Chiner and Jap-pan learning everything they had to teach me, then I come up here and got me the kind of degree you young folks understand. The Parsons School of Design. So don't you worry none about my credentials."

"Well. Okay, here's a key." The voice that uttered

those utterly reckless words was strange, yet familiar. It was her own voice. That's why she recognized it.

Hope promised herself she'd call the insurance company first thing in the morning. Have an art appraiser out. Determine the current value of the African head and the glass bowl. Adjust the insurance accordingly. And when this nonsense was over, she'd hire a proper Manhattan decorating firm to undo the damage.

She would never see Sheila again.

And tomorrow night she was going out with Sam Sharkey.

A little thrill shot straight down through the center of her body just thinking about it.

SAM GUESSED he'd been looking for a brown-haired woman with green eyes and a face to match.

As he stepped out of the luxurious Lincoln he'd hired for the evening, he scanned the crowd surging through the doors of the office building into the blustery wind of December and didn't find anyone who fit that description. The woman who waved and stepped briskly toward the limo was something else again.

"Hope?"

She smiled. "Am I late?"

"Right on time."

First thing, her face wasn't green. Of course he hadn't really expected it to be. He wasn't prepared, though, for creamy skin or full, glistening lips, for the even thicker, darker lashes that framed her eyes—still green, thank God. And her hair. Why had he thought it was brown? Must have been wet. This woman had hair the color of copper pipe.

Maybe she'd dyed it to match her product.

Under a thick, soft-looking cape, she was wearing a

tuxedo. So was he, but the only similarity was their satin lapels. Hers had a short skirt, for one thing, and some kind of low-necked black-lace top under the jacket instead of a white shirt and bow tie. And the jacket poofed out at the top and in at the waist in a way that almost made him forget the reason she was with him in the first place.

For a second he felt like somebody had gut-punched him.

He slid into the car first and let the driver help Hope in beside him. He helped her shrug off the cape—cashmere, by its feel—and pretty soon she was showing him a pair of long, long legs with smooth, slender knees in sheer black stockings. Something bubbled up inside him that was supposed to simmer, covered, for another five years or so, until he really got his feet on the legal ground.

The next thing she was showing him was a laptop. "I hope you don't mind," she said, perching it carefully on top of those pretty knees. "I was into something important when I realized it was time to change jackets."

"Be my—" he paused to clear his throat "—guest. I brought work along, too."

Even before he got to that last line he was looking at her profile, at a big emerald earring on a really cute ear that had a thick bunch of shiny hair tucked behind it, at slim hands with long fingernails painted a sort of ginger-peachy color that matched her lipstick, fingernails that went tap-tap, tap-tap-tap on the computer keys.

Wondering if this had been a really bad idea instead of a really inspired one, Sam reached down for his briefcase.

For a time they rode—sat absolutely still, rather, in

the crosstown traffic—in silence except for her taps and the rustle of the brief he was scanning.

Hope knew it was a brief because she'd let her gaze stray once too often in his direction, sweep up and down the considerable length of him. Lord help her, he was glorious in black tie! Black tux, onyx studs in the buttonholes of a dazzling white shirt, black hair, black lashes...she wouldn't mind having a brief of her own to fan herself with.

She'd set up her laptop at once in order to have something to focus on besides him, but she wasn't getting a lot done. For one thing, she was concentrating on hitting the laptop keys with the pads of her fingers, not her nails. Clear polish was definitely the way to go, and that's the way she usually went, but for some reason she'd wanted to look especially, well, pretty tonight.

But only because she wanted to be sure she left the right impression with the boss's wife. *Lick your lower lip at somebody else. He's mine!*

"How do you want me to act tonight?" she said. She'd been thinking about it, but she hadn't meant to say it aloud.

"Oh, I don't know." Sam rolled the brief a little in his hands and frowned. "Like a girlfriend, I guess."

Wonder how a girlfriend acts. I haven't been one since...

She couldn't remember since when. That was pathetic. Her sophomore year in college, she thought, when she'd dated a pimply philosopher.

"Like...smile up at you, and..."

"We should use terms of endearment," Sam said. "You know, 'Sam, darling, would you fetch me one of those adorable caviar canapés.' That kind of thing."

"I take it I can put 'that kind of thing' in my own words," she said, giving him a sidelong glance.

"Whatever makes you comfortable."

Comfortable? She was already not comfortable and she hadn't even begun acting yet. "We shouldn't try to pretend we've been together a long time," she said to get back on track. "I'm popping up for the first time, and these people know you. You'd have said something about having a girlfriend."

The thoughtful look that crossed his face told her that maybe he would've, maybe he wouldn't. What he said was, "Could we claim love at first sight?"

"What about—" she did little quotation marks with her fingers "—fourth or fifth date, but we feel this really strong attraction?"

He nodded. "That's the attitude. The overdone 'how can I make you happy' stuff, like 'are you cold, here's your cape, are you hot, let's go out on the balcony, are you thirsty, I'll get you a drink.'"

"Very good," Hope said. "Then we do the sudden looks of appreciation at discovering something new about each other we'd never known before, like 'you sail? Oh, my goodness gracious! I simply lo-ve sailing.'"

"That'd be you," he said, looking uncertain for the first time, "saying 'my goodness gracious, I simply lo-ve...'"

"Probably not," said Hope. "But better me than you, now that I think of it. Incidentally, is there something you do that I should know about?"

"I work."

"Well, yes, but..."

"That's it. I work. Just say 'he works.' Anybody you're talking to will know we're well-acquainted."

There was a faint bitterness in his tone, or had she imagined it. Must have, because almost immediately he turned to her with a quick, flashing grin. "Then there's the 'isn't she wonderful' face," he said. "For me, that'd be a sappy smile." He demonstrated.

"Yuck. You look like a lovesick gander. For me," she said, "it would be a sort of parted lips, widened eyes kind of thing." She demonstrated, embellishing her act by pouting out her lower lip as if it were swollen with lust.

He cleared his throat again. She hoped he wasn't getting a cold. "By George, I think we've got it."

"Sorry I interrupted your work," Hope said.

"No problem," he said.

She returned to her laptop and he returned to his brief. But first he had to flatten it out, he'd had it rolled up so tightly.

"CHARLENE." Sam bowed slightly. "Phil. This is Hope Sumner."

"I'm sorry about the circumstances that brought us here," Hope said, looking properly funereal, "but thanks for letting us join you at the last minute. Sam has told me so much about you."

Sam gave her a look. Where did she learn to do that, get all the right words into one receiving-line sentence?

"*We're* delighted that you were willing to join us on such short notice," said Charlene. A pair of huge blue eyes shot daggers in Hope's direction, then Cupid arrows at Sam. He pretended not to notice, but it was hard not to notice that Charlene's dress went down to *here* and came up to *there*, and that she was as voluptuous here as she was slender there.

Silicone at the top and liposuction at the bottom? He'd ask Hope what she thought.

"*Please* come in," Charlene went on. "Make yourselves comfortable. You know almost everybody."

"Yes, yes," Phil murmured. "Sad time for all of us, but I know Thaddeus would have wanted us to go on with our— Harry!" he said, putting a manicured hand forward. "Great to see you. How's the golf?"

Sam gripped Hope's elbow and propelled her forward into the Carrolls' magnificent reception room, a marble-floored space with twenty-foot ceilings and fifteen-foot windows. They ran directly into Cap Waldstrum. "Cap," he said heartily. "This is Hope Sumner." He paused. "You remember Hope."

"No," Cap said, "and I promise you I would've." The caressing gaze of Sam's colleague—his opposite number in the Corporate Department, the man who might edge Sam out of the partnership—slid down to Hope's cleavage. This drew Sam's gaze in the same direction, toward creamy breasts just barely peeking out above the lace.

He had a brief, satisfying daydream of socking Cap in the jaw. And not merely because Cap was apparently an early invitee to this dinner party while he, Sam, was just filling in. This was bad news.

He'd decided to try bluffing Cap about Hope, but as direct as lawyers were, subtlety was out of the question. He'd have to hit Cap over the head with the message to back off.

"I'll get you a drink, *darling,*" he said.

"I'd love some sparkling water, *angel,*" she answered him, giving him the sappy smile he'd thought he was supposed to use. "With lime. I do better if I start out slowly," she was explaining to Cap as Sam made a beeline for the bar, "especially during the holidays."

The bar being a *mano-a-mano* scene, he barely got

back to Hope in time to hear her say, "Pipe. I'm in pipe."

"Not Palmer," Cap said, sounding amazed. "What a coincidence. Our firm—"

"She knows," Sam said abruptly. "Small world, huh?"

"So how did you two meet?" Cap was looking increasingly interested.

"I met Sam through..." Hope began.

"...mutual friends," Sam interjected smoothly. "And for once, the friends had heads on their shoulders." He gave Hope a replay of the sappy grin she'd blatantly stolen from the script they'd agreed on.

"Well, so nice to meet you." Cap The Snake slithered off into the crowd to offer his apple to someone more vulnerable. Sam The Shark decided to let him go...this time.

"Two down," Hope hissed. "Who's next?"

"Not a new player," he hissed back. "Charlene's coming back for a second match."

"Sam," Charlene purred, "you're my dinner partner this evening. Your friend..."

"Hope," Sam supplied. "Hope Sumner."

"Hope Sumner," Charlene said, "will sit across from you between Cap—you've met Cap—" her gaze flitted briefly in Hope's direction "—and Ed Benbow."

"So it's time to go in to dinner?" Sam said, relieved that Charlene hadn't yet invited him to dally with her in some "private" location until the soup was on.

She gave him a mischievous look. "Soon, you impatient boy. Ed," she said, "come and meet..."

"Hope," said Hope.

"Sumner," said Sam.

"Sad occasion we've got here," said Ed. He did some appropriately lugubrious head shaking.

Hope turned suddenly to Sam, "Daring, I didn't ever meet..."

"Thaddeus," Sam supplied.

"Fine man," Ed rumbled. "Salt of the earth."

Sam slid a possessive arm around Hope's shoulders. "We poured him into our opponents' wounds," he murmured.

It was important, of course, to behave as if he and Hope were lovers. About to be lovers, at least. But when she leaned into him, when he felt her shiver of pleasure, he wondered if putting his arm around her and whispering so directly into her ear, a small, very pretty ear, had been a good idea. That shiver had been disquieting, had awakened the sleeping monster inside him again. Except it wasn't inside him. It was right out there in front for all the world to see. And for all he knew, Hope was just ticklish.

"How long have you known our boy Sam?" Ed asked Hope.

"Just a few weeks." Hope smiled prettily. "Long enough to know all he does is work."

"That's Sam, all right," Ed agreed.

Sam had let his hand begin to move against Hope's shoulder in the most natural lover-like way—just testing for signs of response from her—when to his annoyance he felt something tugging at his other arm.

"Sam," Charlene said, "I want to show you my new orchid." She dug her spiky little heels into the floor and tightened her death grip on his elbow. "We can give Ed and..."

"Hope," said Sam, sending a desperate glance in her direction as he slid away from her.

"Hope a chance to get acquainted."

"I'd love to see your orchids," Hope said warmly. "You, too, Ed? You interested in orchids?"

"My wife is," Ed said. "Tanya?"

A stunning blonde half Ed's age left the group she was visiting with and came over to him. "What, honey? Hi," she said, holding out her hand to Hope, "I'm Tanya Benbow. Hey, Shark! What's up?"

"We're going to see Charlene's orchids," Ed said. "Knew you wouldn't want to miss that."

The merry party set out for the conservatory, led by Charlene. Earlier, her slim hips had swung seductively inside her lace sheath. Now she gave the impression of a woman on a forced march.

Sam caught Hope's eye and winked.

3

SNUGGLED IN HER CAPE, standing on the crescent-shaped entryway to her apartment building, Hope said, "Tonight worked out pretty well, didn't it?"

"Don't sound so surprised." He smiled reminiscently. "When Charlene's toes were climbing up my leg and you attacked them with your foot...that was your finest hour."

"It was a stretch from where I was sitting." She watched his smile widen. It set her heart to pounding. "I think I gave Ed a little thrill with my knee, but it was worth it."

"That look you gave Charlene." He shifted into a generic-female falsetto that didn't sound a bit like her, but did sound pretty cute coming from him. "'Find your own leg to climb, you hussy.'"

She remembered the moment entirely too well. She'd had to work steadily at her computer all the way home to distract herself from the sensation that had climbed up from her toes as they caressed Sam's muscular calf beneath the table, a tingly feeling that had made her wriggle against the seat of the dining chair. "Yes. Well worth it," she murmured. "But she does do great orchids."

His low laugh was like warm syrup in the cold night.

"So thanks for a really interesting evening," she said.

He took her hand, held it lightly. "I hope we'll have more of them."

She hesitated. "Let's take it a step at a time, okay? Tonight was successful. Now let's try my milieu."

His smile grew warmer. "Sure. When?"

"Next Wednesday night. My boss and his wife are having their big holiday party then."

"Will you be wearing a mask?" His mouth twitched at the corner.

She really wished he'd stop doing that. It had a strange effect on her, made her twitch in turn somewhere deep down inside in a way that was distracting and unnerving. "Of course not. What do you mean, a... Oh. The masque." The pressure of his hand sent an arrow of heat up her arm. From her shoulder it would spread to her throat, across her breasts. "No," she said abruptly. "The masque is Thursdays and Sundays."

"But..."

"Don't start with me about my schedule." There had to be a way to get her hand back without making a scene. But his hand felt so warm around hers. "So good night, Sam. See you Wednesday." She tugged a little, got free, felt relieved, then deserted and a bit chilly.

"I'll pick you up here." He paused, looking thoughtful. "You did a great job tonight. I don't suppose there's a manual on arm-candy skills..." He took a look at her face. "No, I guess not."

With a wave he slid back into the limo. Before he vanished behind the tinted glass, he flashed her a thoroughly wicked smile.

Hope turned toward the apartment entrance. Her feet were killing her. Funny, she hadn't noticed while Sam was still around.

"Night, Rinaldo," she said to the doorman as she

hobbled into the lobby and summoned the elevator. Almost home, such as it was.

She hadn't been acting. It had been fun being Sam's clinging vine for an evening. He was a hunk with charm and brains and a goal in life. He'd been a sparkling conversationalist during dinner. The boss's wife wasn't the only woman to send an envious glance in Hope's direction.

She felt she was close to agreeing to the arrangement, throughout the holiday season, at least.

But only if she could keep her emotions under control. When their knees accidentally touched, when he cradled her elbow or she took his arm, when their shoulders brushed and a warm, fuzzy feeling began to fluff up inside her, when his utterly charming smile came in her direction, seeming to be for no one but her, she'd wondered if she could keep her quick response to him in perspective. What woman wouldn't respond? He was a very good-looking, a very *masculine* man.

But when he'd put his arm around her, caressed her shoulder, whispered words into her ear... Even now, she could feel the warmth of his breath, the ache that had spread through her, had made her snuggle into him, wanting more. The sense of urgency she'd felt had led her to ditch wondering about perspective and leap directly to worrying. Especially about the sex thing. He hadn't brought it up again. Maybe it had slipped his mind. She wished it would slip hers.

As soon as she opened the door of her apartment, the night view of the New York skyline greeted her through the windows across the room. It always calmed her, made her feel serene and happy. Actually, what it did was justify the savings she'd plundered for the down payment, her huge monthly mortgage and the maintenance expenses.

She didn't turn on the light at once. She wanted to relish the quiet of the moment, give herself time to think about the evening, to think about Sam.

She tossed her briefcase over the top of the sofa as she always did, then reached down to pull the shoes off her aching feet and heard the heart-stopping, stomach-clenching, career-ending clang of a five-thousand-dollar-extra-long-life-battery laptop hitting a hardwood floor.

With a shaking hand, she flipped on the light switch and screamed. An intruder was in her apartment, a creature swathed entirely in black!

A second later she slumped against the door. What a relief! It was herself she was seeing, reflected in the mirror that hung beside the window, a mirror which hadn't been there this morning.

The sofa was gone, though. No, the sofa wasn't gone, it was just in a different place.

Maybelle had made a preemptory strike. But it didn't look as though she'd stolen anything. It looked like she'd added stuff.

Hope came to sudden attention. How could she have forgotten her laptop for even a second? Kicking off her shoes, she grabbed up the briefcase, whipped out the injured team member and ran with it to the sofa. She put it down on the coffee table, sent up a brief prayer and turned it on.

The computer did all its usual beeps and lights, and there was her marketing presentation, safe and sound. The breath she'd been holding whooshed from her lungs. She thanked her lucky stars she'd sprung for the optional two-hundred-dollar computer case with the shock-absorbing extra padding built in. With her next breath, she almost suffocated from the scent that rose from her briefcase.

The laptop had survived, the bottle of Shalimar in her makeup kit had not. But what was a quarter-ounce of Shalimar compared to the product of fifty hours of work?

Strong, that's what it was.

With a feeling of having survived an attack from all sides, Hope collapsed against the sofa. Ummm. She wiggled her toes. Then she looked at the room.

She frowned. The sofa was on the diagonal, facing the little foyer. That was dumb. People came to her apartment to see the view, not the front door. The two squashy taupe armchairs flanked the sofa, also facing the front door.

At least the other two chairs, the antique ones the dealer had called *fauteuil*, the ones he'd warned her were not really for sitting in but were a terrific investment, faced the view. *Great, Maybelle, just great.*

Feeling rebellious, Hope struggled up from the sofa, which seemed to cling to her just as she'd clung to Sam. She crossed the room to sit in one of those chairs whether it liked it or not. Yes, the two chairs faced the view. It was also true—she moved to the other chair just to be sure—that each one looked directly into one of two mirrors that flanked the huge picture window. The mirrors not only reflected her, but also the front door. And the kitchen door. And the bedroom door.

What was this door fetish?

For a minute she sat there, bolt upright, which she'd assumed was the only way you *could* sit in a *fauteuil*, then felt herself start to settle in, lean a little against one of the sculpted wooden arms, rest her head against the faded, faintly dusty, original needlepoint upholstery.

What did the antiques dealer mean, a *fauteuil* wasn't for sitting in?

Enough of this. She was exhausted.

She emptied her briefcase and set everything out in her office, a small alcove off the living room, to air. The Shalimar had to fade by Monday. If it didn't, she would have to announce a new marketing trend—the scented memo.

The message light was blinking on her phone-fax-copier-scanner-answering machine—next year's model would probably have a built-in curling iron. She pushed "Playback."

"Hey, hon! Maybelle!"

Maybelle was one person who didn't need to identify herself on the phone. Hope reeled at the screech, then turned down the volume.

"I made a good start today," the shrill voice continued. "Didn't get no further than the parlor, because I was wanted by the police..."

Hope stiffened.

"...department to juggle the Chief's office around a little."

Hope relaxed. The New York Chief of Police was into feng shui? She hoped the *Daily News* didn't get wind of it.

"Anyhoo, I got them mirrors at the Housing Works Thrift Shop, so you're only out fifty bucks so far. Don't give it a thought. We'll settle up later. I sure hope you're not one of those people who throws stuff onto the sofa soon's she walks in the door, because I moved it. Throwing stuff on the furniture isn't good for you speeritch-ully anyways. We'll talk more about that later.

"Well, you try to get some rest. Soon's I get the Chief and a coupla other clients squared away I'll be back to work on your bedroom, have you sleeping good pretty soon. Oh, would you puh-leeze tell that doorman of yours to let me in next time without putting me through all that hassle?

"Night, hon."

The message had come, her machine-which-never-lied said, at 11:00 p.m. Maybelle sounded like a woman who'd had a whole lot of fully leaded coffee.

Hope went to her bedroom, took off her clothes and hung them up. She'd left her daytime black-and-white tweed jacket at the office. Thank goodness. If she hadn't, it would be permanently Shalimarred just like her briefcase.

She put on a soft flannel granny gown, washed her face, brushed her teeth. She turned down the bed, then stared at it. It stood against the wall just inside the door, facing the view. Nighttime Manhattan twinkled at her from a picture window like the pair in the living room. Already, the week after an early Thanksgiving and not even December yet, the Empire State Building was red and green for Christmas.

About to slip between the sheets, she paused. As tired as she was, it would be lovely to wake up to coffee set on a timer and already made. Yes. She'd sit on the sofa in the living room and have coffee while she read the newspaper.

And stared at the front door.

She tried it out on the way to the kitchen. Weird.

She passed the sofa again on the way to her bedroom, walked over to it, plumped it with her hand.

Maybe she'd pick up one of the magazines that had come today and just rest here a minute before she actually went to bed. She felt so wired, it might get her in the mood for sleep. She'd get that soft mohair throw to put over her feet. And a real pillow from the bed.

It seemed no more than a second later when she woke up to the slap of the *New York Times* against her door and the smell of freshly brewed coffee. Her body buzzed a little with sleepy warmth and something else, something deeper, something achier. She realized she'd been dreaming of Sam.

WHEN SHE ran into Benton in the hallway on Monday, he got as far as, "Morning, Ho—" before deep coughs racked his body and he hurried away with his face buried in his white handkerchief.

At noon on Tuesday, when she went into the executive café in search of an iced tea, she discovered a sign posted on one side of the dining area: "Perfume-Free Zone."

At two that afternoon, a group of her colleagues made shadows outside her door without really showing their faces. "Has to be Hope's office," one said much too loudly. She recognized the oily-smooth tones of St. Paul the Perfect.

"She does have a certain aura about her," said a feminine voice, which then dissolved into a giggle as the shadows vanished.

Ha, ha. Now that she'd become the office joke she'd have to break down and buy a new two-hundred-dollar padded case. The current one had soaked up Shalimar like a femme fatale dying of thirst in the desert.

It was only good-natured kidding, of course. But

Paul Perkins, his real name, wanted this vice presidency as much as she did, and Palmer vice presidents were not office jokes. If she told them what happened—she'd brought the perfume to the office because she was spending the evening being arm candy, then broken the bottle because she'd tossed her briefcase onto a sofa a Texas-born-and-bred feng shui decorator had moved—she could think of that vice-presidency as nothing more than...

Ah. Yes. *A pipe dream.*

But perfume problems faded from her mind in the middle of the afternoon when her computer, which had performed several random tricks during the day, gurgled twice and froze. So much for the two hundred dollars worth of padding. Resigned to the inevitable, she picked up the phone.

"Tech Support." The voice was laconic, sending the message, "Just try to get tech support out of me."

"I'd like to report a homicide," she said briskly.

"Desk or laptop."

"Laptop."

"Bring it down."

"Wait!"

Silence. "Yes?"

"I can't just hand it over to you. I need it. I can't do without it." She was having a panic attack just thinking about it.

"Then you shouldn't have beaten up on it." Sigh. "Bring it down, we'll put your stuff on a zip disk and give you a loaner to use."

"Oh. Oh, well, okay. Wait!" she yelled again.

"What!" Testy this time.

"Aren't you supposed to do the traveling around the

building with the computers and the zip drives and the..."

"How soon do you want it?"

"Immediately."

"You better come on down."

She wouldn't take this kind of cavalier treatment from anyone else in the company. But the tech support group—an ungovernable collection of green-haired, jeans-clad cretins, some of whom had yet to be persuaded that deodorant is our friend—were different. They were geniuses. The entire company relied on them totally and treated them rather like rebellious can't - teach - them - a - thing - but - we'd - never - give - them - away pets.

Grumbling, Hope slid back into her shoes, straightened her black skirt and cream blouse and picked up the laptop. Forget the case. She couldn't take the kind of grief the tech group would give her about the Shalimar. Peeking into the Marketing Department reception area, she found the shared administrative assistants looking not merely busy, but somewhat harried. Okay, she'd take it down herself.

"THIS IS THE LOANER?" she said, gazing in disbelief at the battered object Slidell Hchiridski had just shoved across a counter toward her. The case he shoved along next, which must have cost in the neighborhood of fifteen dollars, appeared to be covered in cat hair. But with an instrument like this one, she supposed it didn't matter.

"Yep," Slidell said. "Works fine. Abusers can't be choosers. Your computer looks like you threw it at somebody." He gave her an accusing glare.

"It was a terrible and tragic accident resulting from

circumstances beyond my..." *Oh, shut up,* she told herself. These were hardly the pearly gates and Slidell was hardly St. Peter. He'd gelled his hair into purple spikes, for one thing, turning himself into a Statue of Liberty with attitude. The company had assigned him to the front desk because of his interpersonal skills. It made Hope shudder to think what lurked behind the double doors that hid the computer lab where the real work got done.

"It's twice as heavy as mine," she protested. "It's a generation older."

"Mr. Quayle didn't gripe when he used it."

"Benton Quayle used this computer?"

"Yep. Until his new one came in."

"Was it in this case?" Hope picked gingerly at the cat hair with two Sunday-night-manicured fingertips.

"Nope. The cat had her kittens in this case."

"You have a cat back there?" She peered around Slidell hoping to get a peek at it.

"Want to make something of it?"

"No." She paused. "I just wanted to see it." She paused again. "I'm thinking of getting a cat. If yours has kittens..."

"The kittens have been assigned to caring homes." He removed a zip disk from the drive, slapped it into a case and shoved it at her. "Person treats a computer like you do shouldn't be trusted with a cat."

Thoroughly humiliated, Hope slunk back to her office to engage in the subclerical task of copying files from the zip disk onto the loaner.

The words of her favorite professor in the MBA program came back to her verbatim: *Turn each challenge into an opportunity.*

Not a day went by that she wasn't grateful to Profes-

sor Kavesh. Those words alone had pressured her
through more than one elbow joint and whooshed her
up to her present level in the company. So instead of
griping about her broken computer, she'd take this opportunity to look at her old files and delete the ones
that were just using up space.

A directory titled "Magnolia Heights" caught her
eye and she opened it first. The file in front of her now
was her part of a presentation to the City of New York,
the general contracting firm and a major plumbing
contractor—Palmer's bid to supply the pipe to plumb
the Magnolia Heights Project.

Magnolia Heights was a middle-income housing
project in the Bronx. Palmer had examined the situation in the thorough, plodding way Benton favored
and had come to the conclusion that lowering their bid
in order to win it would bring the company enough
public relations points to offset the reduction in profits.

Hope was proud of her contribution toward the successful bid. The pipe was high-quality plastic, virtually
indestructible. Inventory Control Number 12867. A
special Palmer pipe that had spent years in Research
and Development and had emerged a winner.

Magnolia Heights was to have been trouble-free,
plumbing-wise, for more years than anyone presently
at Palmer would live.

She slumped in her desk chair. Talk about a pipe
dream! The plumbing at Magnolia Heights had been
nothing but trouble since the first resident turned on
the water.

The next file had come to her and all involved Palmer personnel from Sam's law firm, Brinkley Meyers. It
summarized the case against Palmer.

Reading it made Hope dizzy. The residents had organized a class action suit against the City of New York, which in turn was suing the contracting firm that had built the buildings, which was suing the plumbing contractor, who had lost no time in suing Palmer, which was, of course, counter-suing everybody.

Four law firms, millions of dollars, and all because of a few spotty ceilings.

Hope sighed. It must be worse than that. She felt sad for the people of Magnolia Heights who'd moved in with high expectations that hadn't been met. She wished she knew if there were something she could have done differently, but...

She forced herself not to go back to the Inventory Control Number 12867 files. That pipe was invulnerable. Nothing should have gone wrong.

Surprisingly, the computer pinged, the signal for a new e-mail. So Slidell had connected her with the outside world, at least. Her eyes opened wide when she read, "Meet me at six. Usual place. Big problem." It was addressed to Benton and came from CWal@BrinkleyMeyers.com.

Could "CWal" be Cap Waldstrum?

Instinctively she cast furtive glances left and right and then deleted the message. She couldn't let Benton see that someone had read it. A second later she realized that deleting meant Benton wouldn't get the message at all.

How embarrassing. Somehow the loaner was still receiving Benton's e-mail. Better he miss a message than find out she had accidentally gained access to it. She'd pay attention next time, wouldn't open anything that wasn't addressed to her.

By now the tech people had gone home. Tomorrow she'd correct the error. But how could she? Could she really tell Slidell he'd given her access to Benton's e-mail? Because to do that, she'd have to admit she'd read the message.

She didn't know what made her lose her focus for a moment, cause her to glance out the windows at the darkening December night and most amazingly, made her long to go home.

Everything she had to do tonight could be done at home. She could pack up her dinosaur-laptop and the zip disks, pack up the print materials for the presentation she'd make on Friday to a mega-conglomerate who needed pipe, and settle down at her desk—no, on the sofa—to finish her day's work.

She might even... No, too much trouble. Well, maybe not. She might skim through Zabars to pick up some nibbles and something for dinner with a tad more character than the aluminum-foil-packed dinners that filled her freezer. She might even open a good bottle of wine and indulge in a glass.

What would really be nice would be for someone to call and say they didn't have anything for dinner, and did she, and it would be especially nice if that someone were Sam...

More pipe dreams. She was simply having one of her rare moments of...of... She guessed you'd call it loneliness.

But she'd be getting home two hours earlier than she'd ever gotten home on a Monday night—for no special reason. It was something to mention in passing to Faith and Charity.

really could had given her cause to question
herself. Damn, to do that she'd have to know what she'd
read the message.

She didn't know what Hope had told him. John Gran-
ison came past her to look out the windows at the
gardens. I'm more worried about my employees than
her lover, go home.

4

BENTON QUAYLE, CEO of Palmer Pipe, gave Sam one of
those bone-crushing handshakes and size-you-up
looks men give each other while the women are trad-
ing air-kisses and rating each other's clothes, shoes and
hair. "Sam Sharkey," Benton mused. "That's the sort of
name you don't forget. Seems like I've heard it recently."

Sam nodded. "Could be. I'm at Brinkley Meyers."

"Ah." A thousand words passed silently between
them in that one "ah." "Are you involved in our unfortunate Magnolia Heights case?"

"Not directly."

Hope watched another thousand words zoom between the masculine brains. She wondered how they
did it.

Benton snapped his fingers. "I know who you are.
You're the hotshot litigator they told me about. The
Shark."

Sam smiled. "When a lawyer has a name like mine
it's hard not to get nicknamed 'The Shark.'"

"Yes. Well." After another long, assessing stare at
Sam, Benton turned to Hope. "So you're a friend of The
Shark's?"

Hope had begun to feel left out. This was her party
after all. "No, Benton, I'm one of your employees. In
Marketing. The Shark is my friend."

Fortunately, Benton laughed. "She has such a sense of humor, hasn't she? One of her strengths."

Hope blinked. She knew she had a sense of humor—you had to have a sense of humor when you had sisters who were dingbats—but she thought she'd kept it pretty well hidden at the office.

"Ruthie, this is Sam Sharkey," he said to his wife, "and you know Hope."

"Sam." Ruthie, a pretty, plump woman, held out a glittering hand. Cut off Ruthie's hand, take it to a pawn shop and you'd be set for life. "So lovely to have you both here. Are you *from* New York? No? Ne-*bras*-ka. *Really*. Omaha, by any chance? Palmer has a branch in Omaha. Big market for irrigation pipe, I think. You'd have to ask Benton."

"Hope," she said next, with more warmth than she'd ever shown to Hope. Not even the man's wife could imagine Hope would sleep with Benton to get the vice presidency if she had Sam to sleep with.

Fortunately, Ruthie's gaze went right back to Sam, because the very thought, the highly inappropriate thought of sleeping with Sam was sending flushes of heat all the way down through Hope's cleavage. Feeling her breasts swell, her nipples harden against the silk of her dress, she tossed her shawl over one shoulder to hide the evidence.

Benton reached up to clap a hand on Sam's shoulder and edged him away before Ruthie could get her mouth properly open to speak. "Come on, son," he said. "I'll introduce you around. You might need to know some of these guys someday."

That left Hope and Ruthie gazing after their men, Hope surreptitiously fanning herself, Ruthie merely looking puzzled. "They've bonded," Hope explained.

Ruthie held out her hand to another arrival, but kept her other hand on Hope's wrist. "It's the Magnolia Heights thing," she whispered when she'd said *hello* and *he's over there, do go speak to him* to the latest guests. "It's all he thinks about these days."

The words, "Meet me at six. Usual place. Big problem," skimmed through Hope's mind. "The whole thing is unfortunate," she murmured. "Because whatever the problem is, it can't be the pipe."

"Are you that sure?" Ruthie sounded worried.

"The pipe is invincible," Hope said. Her confidence went down deep into her soul. "I suspect the plumbing contractor did it."

"Somebody did it. Have you seen the damage up there?" The genuine concern on Ruthie's face gave her bejeweled façade a new dimension.

"I haven't," Hope confessed. "I suppose I should take a trip up there and see for myself."

"I went with my Junior League group." Ruthie sighed. "It's serious. I've never seen Benton so tense. You'll keep it between us, won't you?" She looked even more worried.

Hope felt both touched and flattered to have gained the woman's confidence. All, apparently, because she'd walked in with Sam. "Of course," she assured her. "Benton's keeping up a good front at the office. No one needs to know he's worrying."

"Darling..."

The voice came from behind her and its ring of desperation was compelling. She turned to find herself nose to bow tie with Sam.

"Ah, there you are," he said, speaking into her hair and undoubtedly blowing her ruler-straight part awry. "I brought you a glass of wine."

If she moved back, she'd step on Ruthie's plump little toes, so she gave herself a second to savor the sensation of being this close to him, to his faint, musky sandalwood scent, to the crisp starch in his pleated white shirt.

Maybe Sam himself wasn't responsible for the edge of excitement that gripped her when he was around, that gripped her even more tightly now. Maybe it was just that growing up with two sisters she hadn't spent enough time with men to take certain things about them for granted. They were different, and she was just now noticing how different.

Noticing was one thing. Reacting in this frivolous feminine way was quite another, and it had to stop.

"Where is this alleged glass of wine?" she asked the perfectly tied bow tie.

"Over your shoulder," he said. "Don't move. And I mean don't move. I came seeking sanctuary." As if they were dancing, he moved them both in a little half-turn and separated himself from her, then handed her a glass of red wine that seemed to have been sloshed a number of times. Further evidence was the crimson splotch on his French cuff.

She took it gratefully. Seeing that her new friend Ruthie had turned her attention to other arrivals, she said, "Want to go hold up that wall over there for a minute?"

"Great idea."

The room was an elegant space apparently decorated by the same firm who'd done Versailles for King Louis the Fourteenth. Sam looked up toward the frieze of angels on the plastered ceiling eighteen feet above him. "I expected a loft," he remarked, "with exposed pipe."

Hope followed his gaze. "I love lofts with exposed pipe," she said. "I looked for one when I got ready to buy, but I didn't have time to handle a big renovation project. And besides—" she turned to him "—it wouldn't have had Palmer Pipe. Palmer was founded in 1950 and the lofts in Soho date back to—"

Sam's stifled snort stopped her from continuing her perfectly sensible and absolutely accurate reasoning process. "Well, anyway, that's why I didn't," she mumbled, scraping one toe against the marble floor.

She cleared her throat and returned to the original subject. "It was interesting the way Benton glommed onto you," she said. "I've never seen him do anything like that. It was like he was trying to win your approval. Most of the time it goes in the other direction."

Sam's expression began the transition toward serious. "It was more like he wanted to get to know me," Sam said. "Or wanted me to get to know him. Like maybe..."

Hope's breath caught in her throat. "Like maybe the Magnolia Heights case is going to court and you'll be involved?"

His gaze deepened and darkened. There wasn't a hint of laughter in his indigo eyes now. "Yeah. Maybe."

Remembering her promise to Ruthie, Hope glanced nervously around. "We shouldn't be talking about it."

"Why not? We're on the same side."

"Well, of course. But..."

"We *are* on the same side, aren't we? Is there something you know about the case that hasn't been made public?"

Hope suddenly realized this wasn't the smooth, outwardly relaxed Sam she'd been getting to know. She was seeing The Shark for the first time. The impact of his piercing eyes sent a thrill of impending danger through her body. Not danger to her. She had nothing to fear. But danger to whomever might oppose him.

Her new uncertainties buzzed her again like a horde of bothersome hornets. *Big problem. Have you seen the damage up there? I've never seen Benton so tense.*

"All I know," she said with the confidence she felt, "is that 12867 is a virtually perfect product. Something must have gone wrong in the installation."

"You called it by name," Sam said. The laughter reappeared, lightening his eyes, giving them glints of stardust. "You called a pipe by its first name."

"Oh, stop it," Hope said crossly.

Smooth as silk, The Shark glided away into the night and Sam the Social Animal was back.

When Hope saw who was edging his way toward them, she wished The Shark had hung around for a few more minutes. Without thinking, she whispered, "Kiss me."

His startled expression, the blink of his dark lashes filled the nanosecond before his mouth came down to hers, lightly, his lips moving over hers in a soft, persuasive caress. She closed her eyes against the brief electrical shock of contact, then felt every feminine instinct in her body urging her to return the kiss, to deepen it, to let the pure pleasure of it flow over her...

"Hope, hi. Sorry to interrupt."

...to be replaced suddenly by an intense displeasure. She had to force herself to pull away from Sam. His lips clung to hers, too, and his eyes were unreadable as he turned toward the intruder.

"Paul," she said. "How very nice to see you." Anyone else would have skulked away from a couple kissing, which was the outcome she'd hoped for, but not Paul. Still very close to Sam, she felt a rumble emerge from him, suspiciously like the sound of a laugh being swallowed, and she gave him a sharp glance. Or tried to. As soon as she looked at him, she felt like melting.

Oblivious to undercurrents, Paul leaned forward to miss her cheek, then looked expectantly at Sam.

"Sam, this is Paul the...Perkins. Paul Perkins." Someday she was going to slip up and actually call him St. Paul the Perfect to his face. "Shining star of the Marketing Department," she added with a smile and a burst of insincere generosity.

As the men shook hands, Hope managed both to chastise herself for her envy of Paul and grant herself forgiveness. Who had the strength of character, the self-confidence, *not* to be envious of Paul?

Just look at him. Blond hair, an Al Gore face, a nice smile, a firm handshake, square shoulders, squarer personality, a beautiful wife who, although she was intelligent and well-educated, had chosen, *chosen*, mind you, to give up her career in order to provide Paul with a smoothly-run household and two children of extraordinary brains and beauty. Both. If you didn't believe him, Paul had the pictures in the alligator Gucci wallet that matched his alligator Gucci loafers, and if you still didn't believe him, he'd pull out the latest nursery school progress reports, which he just happened to have tucked in the breast pocket of his Loro Piano cashmere suit jacket.

You couldn't help hating him.

Tuning in to the conversation, she observed bitterly that Paul had even taken Sam in. Listen to them. They'd graduated in the same class from Harvard.

They had mutual friends. Paul knew people at Brinkley Meyers. They belonged to his country club.

Bleah!

Paul moved on at last to spread his charm around. Sam lifted two pieces of edible art off the silver tray a member of the waitstaff thrust toward him and hoovered down a shrimp that was wearing a shredded-carrot skirt and a cilantro-leaf hat. "That guy," he said, starting a tiny puff paste skyscraper toward his mouth, "is as smooth as soy milk."

Surprised, Hope stared at him. "Is that good or bad?"

"I can't stand soy milk." He gave her a quick smile. "I shouldn't be so ungrateful. I got a kiss out of it."

Hope blushed. "I'm sorry. I thought…"

"He your competition for the vice presidency?"

"However did you guess?" She slumped despondently against the glazed wall.

"A certain tension I felt in the grip you've got on my elbow."

Hope pulled her hand away as though it had been burned. "Oh, Sam, I am sorry. Did I hurt you?"

"Nothing a little liniment won't cure." But he grinned at her. "Cap's mine," he added.

"Your what?" She'd gotten a little lost in his smile.

"My biggest competition for the partnership. It's different in a law firm. They might decide to offer partnerships to none of us or three of us. On the other hand—" In midgesture he thrust his hand at another passing tray of hors d'oeuvres and came away with two smoked salmon bites, one of which he put directly between Hope's parted lips. "Cap could turn up Number Three, making me Number Four and waiting my turn another year."

"What could he possibly have that you don't?" Experiencing a strange rush of loyalty, Hope mumbled around the smoked salmon.

"A wife."

"Oh, surely in this day and age that couldn't..."

"No. Brinkley Meyers is hardly old-fashioned enough to ask its partners to be married. But what it says about him is that he's settled. His life is organized. Cap can work without wondering when he'll find time to go to the grocery store and take his suits to the cleaners."

"That's what Paul has. A wife." Gloom settled over Hope. Sam nodded. "I see what you mean."

"You should be mingling."

Hope jumped. "Oh, Benton, of course. Sam and I just got involved in a conversation and..."

Benton's indulgent, fatherly smile indicated he'd observed the kiss, and Hope felt the heat rising in her face again. But Benton was smiling. "I know, I know," he said genially. "Take Sam around, though, introduce him to a few more of the folks."

He barreled forward into the crowd, leaving Sam gazing at Hope, looking every bit as puzzled as she felt.

IT WAS LATE when they emerged from the elegant old apartment building where Benton lived and into the relative quiet of the tree-lined side street on the Upper East Side.

"Can we walk for a while?"

He sounded subdued. It worried her, because she still, ages after his kiss, felt like flying. "Sure," she said, making an effort to sound matter-of-fact. "I can catch a cab on Madison."

"Warm enough?"

"Oh, yes." Her words made white clouds like smoke rings in the cold air. His eyes were picking up glints from the streetlights as his gaze flickered over her, then lingered on her face. That look heated her blood, sent it racing through her veins. Yes, she was definitely warm enough.

He took her arm. "Those snow boots look sort of decorative. Do they work?"

Hope glanced down at the suspiciously shiny side-walk, then at her short, heeled boots with their fluffy linings peeking up out of the top. *No. Don't let go of my arm, not for even a second. If you do, I'll fall flat on my...* She leaned into his shoulder. "They're supposed to. I've never actually put them to the test."

Somehow his arm was around her instead of merely linking with hers, and he pulled her a little closer.

"You're not wearing snow boots at all," she said, feeling shorter of breath with every passing second.

"I don't need snow boots. I'm from Nebraska."

"Oh. That makes sense." She smiled up at him, not realizing how close he was until her face brushed his chin. She quickly turned away.

For a few minutes they moved along in silence, Sam matching his stride to hers. Ahead, cars crowded Madison Avenue, lights flashing, horns honking. But walking beneath the frosted trees, down the street of tall, elegant town houses, Hope felt that she and Sam were in a completely different, perfectly serene world.

"I was a big hit at your party," he said at last.

"I was a big hit at *your* party," she reminded him.

"So do we have a deal?" He halted and turned her toward him, looking her squarely in the eyes.

She gazed up at him. How could she say anything but—

"Yes," she said. "It's a deal."

"Sealed with a kiss," he said, and leaned down to capture her mouth with his.

THE BRIEF KISS at the party hadn't been for him, not really. But the reason for it didn't matter. It had whetted his appetite to the point that he would have used any excuse to kiss her again. Still, he'd intended it to be a light, casual kiss, just the merest taste of her to take home with him.

Who was he kidding? He'd begun to want her with an intensity that threatened to take over his life, to want her in a way that was dangerous to his carefully made plans. And now, for a blip in time, he had her.

He moved his lips lightly over hers, feeling her slight shock and his own surprise at the tentative responding pressure from her warm, soft mouth. It was unbearably sweet, her kiss, and it gave him the nerve he needed to let his arms slide around her, his hands to splay against her back, touching as much of her as he could at one time.

As tentative as she was, he slipped his tongue over her full, sensuous lower lip and into the crease of her mouth, almost groaning when she allowed him entrance, welcomed it. Aching with want, he explored, his tongue tangled with hers as they came together in quick consent to seize this moment, almost as if it were stolen, almost as if it could only happen now, might never happen again.

His arms tightened around her, caressing her back in long, desperate strokes, bringing her as close to him as he could, resenting the layers of coats that kept him away from skin that would feel like cream to the touch. His erection, instant and demanding, throbbed insistently and he pressed her against it, trying to ease the ache, only making it worse.

Even through all the layers, he could feel the mounds of her breasts as she pressed them against his chest. Was she aching, too? Was it too much to hope that she saw this moment as something to build on—

Hell, something to finish, and soon. His heart pounded hard in his chest, his head felt light as the blood rushed to his groin, and he poured his whole being into a single kiss she'd never be able to forget.

Unable to resist, he slipped his hands inside her coat and parted it, sliding his arms around her again, brushing her breasts with his fingertips. The low moan that came from deep in her throat added fuel to the fire already burning inside him. He stroked her back, moved lower to her waist, took her mouth more deeply as he molded her to himself. The moan ended in a sigh as she twisted against him.

It was pure torture. Letting her go with nothing more than a kiss was inconceivable, unbearable. He would take her home, and they would make love.

As that thought ran through his barely functioning brain, he realized he was in trouble, agonizingly turned on, nearly out of control, and there was absolutely no chance Hope would let him come home with her and make love. "Love" wasn't part of the deal. They still hadn't even negotiated sex.

It took the most enormous effort of will, but he loosened his hold on her, slowed down the kiss and finally wrenched himself away from her with what he hoped was a sort of method-acting rendition of resigned reluctance. What he wanted to do was bash something. Hard.

Not Hope. What he wanted to do to her was ease her down on a soft surface and bring her to unprecedented heights of ecstasy—in the most primitive way. But that silver Jag parked across the street—it could use a bashing.

Thinking how gentle he'd be with Hope, he slid his hands out from under her coat as slowly as he dared, then pulled the coat tightly around her with one last stroke down the lapels. She gazed up at him, giving him a tremulous smile. Her face was flushed, her mouth looked bruised and swollen.

"And if I default on the contract?" she said, but her voice sounded shaky.

"I got a little carried away," he admitted.

"Tension," she said, nodding.

"Tiredness."

"Long week. It's only Wednesday."

"And it's almost Christmas."

"We have a tendency to overdo at Christmas," Hope said.

"Nobody overdid next week," he said. He'd made himself calm down—how, he didn't know. He could hear real regret—no method acting here—seeping into his voice. "As far as I know, there's nothing on our schedule until a week from Friday night."

"Oh." She didn't sound happy about it either. "I guess that's right."

"Time to catch up on work."

"I can use it."

"Me, too."

The scene was getting silly in Sam's opinion. He didn't want to let her go, and he sensed somehow that she didn't want to let him go, but they both knew that the deal was to let each other go, absolutely, no strings, between their public appearances. He didn't know how she felt, but he *knew* that any addenda to the deal would have to be negotiated. And you didn't negotiate in the heat of passion.

As quickly as he could, he navigated both of them to Madison Avenue and shouted, "Taxi!" so fervently that a cab crossed three lanes of bumper-to-bumper traffic to pull up in front of them.

He helped her into the car over her protests, then tried to hand a ten to the driver, but she grabbed his hand and steered the bill right back into his pocket.

He wished she'd aimed for a pants pocket, and over-shot her mark.

5

"HOW'S IT GOING?"

"Quite well," Hope informed her sisters. She'd finished the newspaper, she'd microwaved a pancakes-and-bacon frozen breakfast, and now she sat cross-legged on the sofa gazing thoughtfully at *Getting a Cat*, a book she'd purchased recently to help her with the all-important adoption decision. "When I feel I'm ready to bring him home, I'm going to a rescue agency. I'm leaning toward a long-haired—"

"Not the cat!" Charity interrupted her.

"Oh. Oh, she's going to work out just fine." Hope snuggled more deeply into the corner of the sofa and glanced out the window at the snowflakes drifting down.

"She?" Faith asked.

"She?" Charity echoed hollowly.

"Why, yes, Yu Wing, the interior..."

"Not Yu Wing." Matching sounds of annoyance came at her through the receiver. "The *man*."

"Oh, him." Hope had known perfectly well which aspect of her life her sisters had called to quiz her about, but they were so cute when they sputtered. "He's very nice. Attractive, too."

Now they were actually holding their respective breaths. Didn't they have anything more important to do than wander like ghosts at the margins of her life?

They'd always had lots of dates. Why weren't they focusing on finding that one special man for *themselves?*

She realized they must be turning blue waiting for her answer. "We've gone to several parties together."

Whoosh! "Did you have fun?"

"Has he kissed you good night yet?"

"No," Hope lied. It wasn't a lie exactly. Sam's kiss hadn't been your standard good night kiss.

"No to which question?" Charity said.

"Kissing me good night is not part of our deal," she hedged. "We see each other on business occasions for business reasons." And it was driving her mad! "Which is exactly the way it's supposed to be," she added, emphasizing that fact to herself more than to her sisters.

"Of course it is," Charity said soothingly.

"Oh, yes," Faith said. "Exactly."

There was a long, pregnant pause before Charity said, "Is he the kind of man you might wish would kiss you good night sometime in the future?"

"She means the distant future," Faith hastened to add.

It was fortunate for all concerned that Hope's call waiting beeped. If it hadn't, she might have burst into tears and told them he'd given her a kiss against which all future kisses would be measured, then loaded her into a taxi and sent her home, a quivering mass of Jell-O that hadn't completely set. "Can't tell you how I've enjoyed talking to you," she said briskly, "but I must take this call. Hello," she said to whomever had delivered her.

"Hope? Sam."

It wasn't fair, the shiver of anticipation that threaded through her body. Only the most desperately deprived

of females could react so strongly to, "Hope? Sam."
Just because she'd been out with the man a few times,
shared a laugh or two, a touch or two and a kiss against
which all future kisses would be measured didn't
mean she ought to be melting like ice cream under hot
fudge sauce at the sound of his voice.

"What's your take on Christmas shopping?"

Hope blinked and sat up straighter. "Pardon me?"

"Would Christmas shopping fit within the parameters of our deal?"

Parameters. Borders. Limits. The limits of the deal.
Now the word "parameters" was making her heart
thud dully against her white cotton sports bra. She was
a pathetic excuse for a woman, she truly was.

"It hadn't occurred to me," she said uncertainly,
"but I suppose the idea is to help each other out, so I
guess..."

"I have some time this afternoon. I like to shop
early."

Early? This was early? She'd done her shopping
months ago.

"It's snowing," she informed him.

"That's the best time."

"Could this be a romantic streak showing up?" As
soon as she said it, she wished she hadn't.

There was a brief pause. "I was thinking the snow
might keep some of the folks home. I hate crowds. Tell
you what. If you'll help me pick out stuff for the
women on my list, I'll treat you to a drink at the Oak
Bar when we finish."

The *women* on his list? She'd imagined him as being
without women. Was he suggesting he had a stable of
bimbos, the empty-headed, spandexed type you could
clean up, but not take anywhere?

She supposed she ought to feel flattered that she was the one he could take *anywhere*. She had a sudden vision of herself and Sam in the elegant old bar, laden with packages, looking like any of the other couples she'd seen collapsed there after a day of strenuous shopping. It made her feel strangely warm inside. *Bimbos, eat your hearts out.*

And she did need wrapping paper.

"I do need wrapping paper," she said.

"Great. I'll meet you at Saks at one."

"The Trish McEvoy counter."

"The who?"

"Okay, just inside the main entrance on Fifth Avenue."

"It's a date."

No, it wasn't a date, Hope reminded herself as she put down her cat book, not as regretfully as she should have, and glanced at her laptop, not as longingly as she should have. It was a business meeting, pursuant to the procurement of inventory. Christmas presents for the women on his list. She could hardly wait to hear who they were.

"THEY'LL LOVE cashmere sweaters. You can never have too many cashmere sweaters. All I'm saying is I don't think you should give all of them the *same* cashmere sweater."

"You don't? It sounded so efficient. Yellow for Mom, pink for Betsy and blue for Kris."

That wasn't how he felt, really. He'd be sending them big checks for Christmas, his parents and both of his sisters. Betsy and Kris would spend the big checks on their kids, or bills. Whatever he sent Mom and Dad seemed to go directly toward presents for his four nephews and the care of Mom's parents.

He wanted his personal gift, the one under the tree, to be something special, but sometimes he felt so helpless, thinking one cashmere sweater, one pair of real gold earrings wasn't going to make the slightest difference in their lives. Still, he'd asked Hope to help and she'd never help again if he didn't listen to her. God, the woman was bossy! But for some weird reason, he liked having her boss him around.

"Okay, what would you buy for them?"

"I need to know more about them," Hope said with an air of patience stretched to the limit.

He liked the way she looked today, too. Black pants tucked into black snow boots, black sweater, probably one of those cashmeres-you-couldn't-have-too-many-of, and a leopard jacket that nobody would take for real leopard. It turned her eyes even greener, her hair even more coppery.

But he was afraid he'd be having the same feelings about her no matter how she looked, and "afraid" was the operative word here. He'd stretched his imagination to the limit to think of a reason to see her today. He would see her next Friday night, and he should have let it go at that. He needed every minute, every second of that time to get over the effect of a perfectly natural, ordinary kiss.

To get back, in fact, to the "spirit of the law" they'd agreed to in their business deal. He'd never in his life closed a contract by kissing his client. Never felt even remotely inclined to.

So what he should have done was concentrate on his work, the way he'd trained himself to do, and not had another thought about Hope until his Palm Pilot reminded him to pick her up on Friday.

Problem was, it hadn't been an ordinary kiss. So instead, here he was, doing his Christmas shopping earlier than he'd ever done it in his life, because he knew that asking her out to dinner or a movie wasn't part of the deal, and ending either of them with another kiss—and more—wasn't either. He knew himself well enough to know that he couldn't handle another kiss like that without demanding more.

He needed to stick to the original rules. She did, too, according to her.

"Your family," Hope said. "I asked for a few details."

She was literally tapping her foot. "Ah," he said, coming around. "Mom's, you know, sort of..." He held his hands out from his hips to indicate that Mom had gotten a little stout over the years. "Betsy's skinny as all hell and Kris is starting to look way too much like Mom."

"Hair color?"

"Gray, blond and blond."

"Eyes?"

"Brown, blue and blue."

"Like yours?"

Sam, who'd been admiring the curve of her mouth with those very same eyes, felt that familiar tingle in his groin, intense enough to make him wonder if he might be able to make partner without concentrating quite so completely on his work. Take time to give in to the tingle every now and then. But he wanted Hope to give in with him, and giving in wasn't on her agenda.

He cleared his throat and looked away toward a sexless pile of turtlenecks. "Yeah, all us kids got Dad's eyes."

"Okay, then, let's see what we have here."

Her small, slim hands rifled through stacks. Her green eyes sent a narrowed gaze toward the displays. "How about this for your mom?" She laid out a bright-red sweater, loose and long, that sort of curled at the neck.

Sam tried to imagine his mother in red. The more he thought about it, the more he thought she might look pretty in a red sweater. She'd wear it all Christmas day. "Good choice," he said. "I'll take it."

"Now Betsy," she said, and came up with a blue, not a light blue, but a medium-sort-of-blue sweater set. The kind that had the sleeveless thing underneath and the cardigan to match. "Two down," he said approvingly, "and one to go."

"Kris."

She had a head for names.

"We want something slenderizing for Kris that doesn't yell 'lose weight.'"

He was offended. "I would never…"

"Of course you wouldn't. You wouldn't have to. She'd be yelling it to herself." Hope busied herself in another stack. "How about this? What this says to me is 'blond bombshell.'" Hope held it up in front of herself.

All it said to Sam was three hundred twenty-five dollars, but he had to admit it was a good choice for Kris. It was black, not exactly a turtleneck, but it came up high under Hope's chin—a small chin, the point of her heart-shaped face, but a strong chin, too.

The sweater. Kris. "Yeah, I think she'd like that."

"The way it's knitted," Hope said, seemingly unaware of his ruminations about her chin, "with these triangles that tuck in a little bit, it'll be slimming. Okay, who's next?" She gazed at him expectantly.

"Well, there's Grandmother Sharkey and Grandmother Ellsworth."

She seemed to relax a little. "Robes, maybe? Or something a little less clichéd? I've got this foot spa..."

"I like it here," Sam said.

"But shouldn't you vary your..."

"I'll give them shawls. I'm happy in this department." She might be bossy, but he wasn't exactly Beta Man himself. "It's not too crowded, nobody's bugging us..."

"Nobody's waiting on us at all."

Hope sent a disapproving gaze at a salesperson. It somehow motivated the woman to scurry toward them burbling, "May I help you?"

"Yes. We'd like these sweaters."

"And maybe some shawls," Sam said.

"Oh, we've got some lovely shawls and capes," the salesgirl said. "Right over here."

"We'll look," Hope said repressively, "while you put these sweaters in gift boxes."

It only took her three minutes to convince Sam that shawls said, "old lady," at least when you gave them to old ladies, and that fuzzy mohair cardigans would make his grandmothers feel younger. "Who's next?" she said, giving him that same expectant look.

Was there something else in that look? Something guarded? Suspicious?

"My cleaning lady and my administrative assistant."

She relaxed again. "Can I possibly talk you out of the

cashmere department and into jewelry or scarves? Or gloves. Gloves are nice."

"Oh, okay," he grumbled. There was some brand of scarf women talked about, just the kind of status symbol the administrative assistant he shared with two other lawyers would recognize and appreciate as an addition to the check he always gave her. His cleaning lady would like finding a pair of warm gloves along with her Christmas check.

"You want to wrap these yourself?"

"Are you kidding?"

"All Saks is going to give you is a gray box and a red ribbon," she warned him. "Or—" she waved a threatening finger "—we can stand in line at the gift wrap kiosk for about two hours. I did that once. In a pinch. I've been careful not to get in a pinch ever since."

Sam weighed his horrible options. "I'm going with the gray boxes and red ribbons," he decided. The truth was, his mother would help him with the wrapping when he went home to Nebraska for Christmas.

"How exactly did you talk me into stopping into F.A.O. Schwartz," Hope asked, embracing an Irish Coffee with both shivering hands.

"You deserved a reward for getting me out of Saks so fast," Sam said. "F.A.O. Schwartz was your reward."

"Ha!" said Hope. "You wanted to play the video games."

"I won." He gave her a supercilious look over the rim of his martini glass, then smiled. "Thanks for going with me. Think the kids are going to like that stuff I got them?"

"How could they not love it? PlayStation consoles,

games galore, those skinny little scooters... They *are* boys, right?"

"All four of them. I saw you sneaking around to the doll section. Sorry."

She flushed. "Just wanted to take a look at the inventory and the display techniques. How old are the boys?"

"Twelve, eleven, ten and nine. Kris and Betsy got married young, had the kids young."

Hope examined the expression on his face. For a moment he'd seemed depressed. "What made you different?"

"Somebody in the family had to have some ambition. Everybody else has the 'all you need is love' philosophy."

"Sometimes I wonder..." Hope began, then fell silent. Sometimes she wondered if that was what happiness boiled down to, simply loving and being loved.

Her biological mother had sacrificed everything for love, had estranged herself from her family when she married the wild, handsome, romantic pilot who had been Hope's and her sisters' father. She'd even sacrificed her life to be with him on the day their father's passion for the sky took them away forever.

But she'd loved her daughters, too. She'd left them, not to her family, but to her childhood friend Maggie Sumner and her husband Hank. While Maggie and Hank might suggest that you needed more than love to live a fulfilling life, it was love that ran their home.

Faith and Charity wanted both, professional success and love, while she'd always felt love was something you couldn't have until you'd achieved the professional success. Now she was starting to wonder.

The Irish coffee—and something else, perhaps—was

sending a comfortable warmth through Hope's insides. She eased back into the leather banquette, relaxed into the dimness of the gracious wood-paneled room. Beyond the windows, the snow fell fast and furious, magnifying and reflecting the tiny lights that wound around the trees from trunk to top and feathered out among the branches. Could there be a better way to spend a wintry afternoon than to watch snow falling on Christmas lights and contemplate love?

Feeling a blush heat her face, she was careful not to look at Sam as she rephrased her question. "What happens to people like you and me to make us put love on the back burner, behind a pot of ambition at full rolling boil?"

"For me, it was my first look at what you can do when you have money. The power that comes with it." His face darkened. "What happens when you don't have it. People may respect you as a person, but in a fight, you're helpless."

It was as though he heard the bitterness in his own voice, as though he were appalled at himself for letting the conversation drift into personal matters. A series of expressions shifted across his face before a curtain dropped to obscure the man inside.

"Wow," he said, "shopping is harder than racquetball."

"Racquetball's your game?"

"Most exercise in the shortest time," Sam said.

"Figures," Hope said, and smiled at him. She welcomed the shift in the conversation. She'd been intrigued by the glimpse of what made Sam run, but she was more than happy to move away from her own thoughts of love.

IN ANOTHER MINUTE he'd have told her the whole sad story of his family's slide from prosperity to bare subsistence. It wasn't the martini talking, either. He hadn't had enough gin to blame it on that. It was the sense of comfortable familiarity he'd felt with Hope almost from the moment of meeting her.

Comfortable talking to her. Uncomfortable in other ways.

He hadn't intended to let himself feel desire for her. He couldn't afford to. He had to stay focused on nailing down his partnership. He couldn't let himself get sidetracked by her warm smile, her occasional blush, the way she'd kissed him, as if she wanted him with something close to the desperate wanting he felt for her.

She couldn't want him as much as he wanted her. Nobody could want anybody as much as he wanted her. God, how long had it been? He'd been a fool to make himself this vulnerable to a woman.

It was dangerous to get so close to her. There were things he didn't want to have to explain to her, like his small, inconvenient, cheap-for-New York apartment. He earned plenty. He didn't want her to know he only spent it on the things he needed to to keep up his successful-and-soon-to-be-more-successful image. There were too many things he had to do before he could relax and admit he was a rich man.

If, God forbid, it didn't happen, he had no intention of being caught unprepared the way his father had been when the crop failed, and failed again, until there wasn't anything to fall back on. His father had ended up working at the local John Deere distributorship, repairing tractors. There were times when all Sam could hear in his head was his mother's voice saying, "But we still have each other. That's all that matters." It was what she said each time she told him and the girls they couldn't afford whatever it was they wanted.

Like college. The girls had gone to work at the beauty shop and the grocery store right out of high school. They'd married local boys when they were way too young, before they'd learned anything about the rest of the world. He'd dared to be different, had worked his butt off to get where he was today, so close to his goal.

The partners would meet just before Christmas to go over their profit-and-loss reports, distribute bonuses and make decisions about new partners. Then he'd know where he stood.

He had to slow things down with Hope. He wouldn't let himself make up another excuse to see her until the party Friday night. He'd remain within the boundaries of the deal they'd made.

Of course, there was that one aspect of the deal they'd never quite finalized.

He was too far gone to kid himself. He wanted to make love with Hope. It had nothing to do with the deal.

But maybe he could convince her it did.

He reached his apartment building, let himself in, climbed three flights of stairs and opened the door to his one-room studio apartment. Dropping his Christmas presents on the bed, he wondered what Hope was doing right now.

HOPE HAD HALF WISHED he'd suggest following up their day of Christmas shopping with dinner, but he didn't, merely mentioned he'd see her next Friday, which made her feel half-relieved. Unaccustomed to feeling half anything, she felt vaguely unbalanced as she stepped through her door into her living room, and knew she couldn't blame the feeling on the unwieldy bag of Christmas wrappings she'd lugged home.

She sensed a difference even as she wisely—she'd learned her lesson—switched on the light before taking another step. In the course of a single afternoon, a tree had sprung up in the corner of the room behind the sofa.

Its small, delicate leaves cast shadows on the ceiling and almost seemed to shade the sofa from the lights of the city beyond the windows, to shelter her from the bustle and noise, to cradle her in its branches.

She put down her shopping bag with a resounding thump. *For heaven's sake, it's just a tree.* Maybelle had struck again.

"WE'RE NOT going to reach settlement in the Palmer case."

Sam leaned back in his chair. "Too much human interest involved. It's really the media's case now."

Phil nodded. "And you know, you can't help looking at it from Magnolia Heights' point of view. Water system's not working right, leaks everywhere, mold, mildew..."

"But we're convinced Palmer's not liable."

"We represent Palmer Pipe." Phil looked at him levelly. "We make our case on the evidence they've given us."

"I realize that," Sam murmured.

Phil sighed. "The truth is, we've had our experts run test after test on that pipe, and it's exactly what Palmer claims it is."

"Number 12867," said in the voice of a fond mother,

came to Sam's mind, and he had to keep himself from smiling.

"The reason I called you in," Phil went on, "is that the Executive Board wants you to head up the litigation team, argue the case in court."

Sam's heart thudded in his chest. "Thanks, Phil, I'm honored."

"This says a lot about how the firm feels about you," Phil said.

He didn't need to be more specific. He was saying the firm was giving the case to Sam because they were seriously considering him for the partnership. Palmer was the pipeline—Lord help him, he was getting as bad as Hope—to his future, to a level of security that might give him the confidence to take the deal with Hope to another level.

"You got Charlene's vote, too," Phil said. "She said you passed her test."

"Test?" Sam tried to hide his embarrassment.

Phil waved a hand. "I don't know what she was talking about either. All I know—" he paused, looking thoughtful "—is that any test Charlene dreams up is going to be damned hard to pass."

"I'm, um, flattered," Sam murmured, ducking his head.

"She was really impressed by Hope Sumner. You still seeing her?"

Sam's head shot up. "Ah. Yes. That is, we see each other fairly frequently."

"I thought it might be more serious than that." Phil gave him a fatherly glance. "You're Benton's choice to argue the case in court. He tells me Hope's a hairsbreadth away from a vice presidency. It's getting to be like family around here, with Benton and me watching the kids graduate."

This would be a good time to confess to Phil that he and Hope had simply struck a deal. But the image of her came into his mind. Her straight, smooth auburn hair shining like silk as it moved in the cold winter wind and settled back into place at once. Her green eyes shining like jewels as they sat together in the back seat of a limo on the way to a party, planning their strategy. Her slim, neat body in a simple, expensive-looking black dress or suit, her long, elegant legs—the passion that had bubbled up so unexpectedly when he kissed her.

But most of all, the passion for life, the pure energy that emanated from her. She'd be a great woman to come home to. All he had to do was convince her that's where she needed to be—at home, waiting for him.

No, that was too much to ask. They could work something out, though, if— "It's too early to say anything," he said, getting up to leave, knowing it was time. He smiled at Phil. "You'll be the first to know. Thanks again, Phil. I'm excited about this case. I'll clear my decks and get right on it."

"I HAVEN'T forgotten you, hon." Maybelle's voice shrilled incongruously into the hush of the office where Hope gazed with growing concern at her borrowed laptop.

Hope jerked her attention away from the screen. "Oh, I know," she said absentmindedly. "I've been busy, too. Incidentally, I was rather expecting a bill from you."

A predictable snort came from Maybelle. "Plenty of

time to settle up," she said cheerfully. "I'm a little slow on this billin' stuff. My clients don't seem to mind."

"I'm sure they don't." Even worried, Hope couldn't help smiling. "The tree's nice," she added.

"Glad you like it. In fact, I called to tell you I'm bringin' a few more little things by this week. Okay with you if I just pop in and out?"

Since Maybelle had consistently added to Hope's inventory—free, to date—rather than carting things away, she had lost her fear of burglary. "Sure. I'll tell the doormen."

"Well, them and me's gettin' along much better since I talked the super into fixing up a little coffee room for 'em in the basement," Maybelle said. "These cold days—" a shiver sound came from the speaker phone "—a little hot coffee on their breaks makes 'em happier than a raise."

Hope stared at the desk phone as Maybelle rang off. She wondered if the woman slept, or ate, or did anything, in fact, except organize lives and drink coffee.

But then her gaze went right back to the screen, which was filled with Benton Quayle's unread e-mail messages.

Half of them, easily, were from "CWal" and someone at the plumbing contractor's company who was identified only by a number and the firm's name.

She was in a quandary. Because she'd opened that one message and deleted it, Benton had probably missed a meeting and must have inferred something was wrong. She hadn't opened any more of his messages, but she couldn't keep herself from staring at the sheer volume of conversation going on between Benton, Sam's competitor Cap Waldstrum and someone from the plumbing firm that had laid the pipe in Magnolia Heights.

Merely detail work, she was sure. Related to the case, undoubtedly. Even that first message could have indicated nothing more than a missing invoice, something simple like that. But why a special meeting place?

Hope chewed her lip and worried. One thought lightened her spirits. Tonight she'd see Sam again.

The week had seemed like a century.

6

HE'D KEPT his promise and spent a week away from Hope, but instead of helping him calm down, it had given him too much time to think about her.

Mainly he'd thought about how to present his current state of raging lust in the reasonable terms of a man who was merely involved in an arrangement, an arrangement whose boundaries he deeply desired to expand.

Explode was more like it. Because that's what he was going to do if he couldn't convince her that sex with rules was better for both of them than sex without rules. That sex would be a sensible thing between them because they both knew the rules. So they would have sex and feel better and less tense, and then their lives would go on as usual.

He didn't have to go very deep into his heart to realize he was talking nonsense. Hope would see right through him.

Unless... Unless she was looking for an excuse, too, some reason she could let herself give in to the womanly needs she had to have. How could she not have them? He had felt the attraction between them when they kissed. It was a rich, deep thing that vibrated the air, warmed his heart, heated his blood. A sensation like that couldn't be unilateral, could it? She had to be feeling it, too.

He was afraid the doorman had caught him talking to himself as he advanced into Hope's apartment building, a warrior determined to claim his prize. At least to give it his very best shot.

SHE'D LONGED for the moment he'd appear at her door all dressed up and ready to go with her to yet another party. As always, his impact was more dramatic than she'd imagined. But one look at him and she knew something had changed. For the first time since they'd met, he seemed uneasy.

Her anxieties went into overdrive. *It's not working for him. My social life is impacting his working time. He's found—oh, please, God, don't let it be that—a woman he actually wants to spend time with, work be damned.*

"I'm trying out a red wine," she said. *No one would ever guess I'm wasted.* "We have time for a glass."

"Fill it to the brim," Sam said.

Hope blinked. Something in his voice made the heaviness deep inside her add weight. It was a struggle to get herself into the kitchen, pour the wine.

"Bad day?" she asked, waiting to hear the worst and at the same time, fighting a crazy desire to throw him down on the sofa and ravish him. Not that she knew how to ravish, or even how to appear ravishable to an experienced ravisher. But she had a sudden interest in learning.

"Interesting day. Interesting week. But..."

But *what?* Her mind, usually so serene and organized, was a jumble of conflicting, irrational sensations. They were too animal to be called thoughts.

He didn't gulp the wine, slam the glass down and bleat, "God, I needed that." Instead, he took a deep, appreciative sip and said, "This is great. Where'd you get it?"

"Burgundy dot com." They were down to that— sharing Web site discoveries.

"I should be able to remember that."

"Is something wrong?" Even in her present condition of mindless lust, she remembered the principle of getting straight to the point.

He frowned. "Not wrong, exactly."

"We'd better talk about it. Clear the air." Thinking hard, Hope came up with a reason to clear the air. "We'll get to the party, people will think we're fighting, treat us like we're about to go on the market again."

Right. Not that I care if you're through with me. I just want to keep up the façade, that's all.

"No, no, it's nothing like that. Quite the opposite."

This time Hope simply waited. They still stood outside the kitchen door. He nudged a small potted plant aside to put his wineglass down on a crescent-shaped table that stood against the wall.

Hope frowned at the table. It used to be square, didn't it?

The mirror sent back a glimpse of his face, its muscles taut, eyes hooded by downcast lashes. "Remember I asked you how you felt about sex?"

Hope felt a stillness come over her as all her energy, all her will, went toward maintaining a serene expression while sensations—a deep, throbbing pleasure, a sharp stab of anticipation, a touch of something that was either fear or excitement—attacked from the inside.

"You didn't really give me an answer, but, well..."

He cupped her shoulders with his hands. She could

feel their heat through the sheer silk of her dress, could feel the power in the fingers that held her so lightly.

"It's been a long time for me."

For me, too. Hope nodded dumbly. *Like never.* She felt her lips parting as anticipation built up inside her—a roiling reservoir behind a dam that threatened to break at any moment.

"Recently," he paused again, "I can't seem to think about anything else."

He meant anything else but sex, not anything else but her. Just because she couldn't think about anything but him didn't mean he felt the same way.

"So I'm asking you again. Can we do this one more thing for each other without...you know..."

"Letting our emotions get in the way?" Her voice sounded rough from disuse. She tried to clear her throat, but it felt too tight to do even that. She turned her head, unable to look him in the eye while she told such an out-and-out lie. "I've been thinking about it, of course. I realized we'd tabled that part of the agenda..." *Oh, Lord, can't I even talk about sex in anything but business-speak?*

"I think we could manage it," she whispered. "If we're careful to keep it therapeutic, not make too much of it."

She felt his closeness and turned back to him. The kiss he'd undoubtedly meant for her cheek took her full on the mouth. His lips were hot on hers, the light brush of his caress searing like a branding iron.

"I want you to enjoy it, too." The words hovered over her lips. His breath was sweet and warm. "It wouldn't be fair if you didn't. This is a mutual thing."

"Oh, let's not worry about..."

He put a hand on each side of her head, threading

his fingers through her hair. "Sh-h-h," he said. "Didn't say I was worried."

Into the silence Hope said, "When?"

"The sooner the better." The edge of laughter under his mock-desperation soothed her a little.

"We're going to be out late tonight." She hesitated. "Max's parties never end." *Things to do! I have things to do before...* "But tomorrow maybe? I'd rather you came here. I'd feel more comfortable, I think."

He nodded. "Thank you. You are a kind, kind person."

Unbelievably, he looked at his watch. "We're going to be later than that polite ten minutes. Are you ready?"

So that's how it was going to be. Therapeutic sex—the concept didn't give him a shred of trepidation.

In self-defense, she looked at her watch, too. "Mind if I make a quick phone call before we leave?"

"Go right ahead. I'm going to write down the name of this wine. I might want to order a case."

She felt like slamming the bedroom door on his words. When she'd closed it behind her, softly, of course, she gritted her teeth and snatched up the phone. It was only fitting that she'd get the answering machine. With an eye on the door, she hissed her message into it.

"Maybelle, I need you *immediately*. You've got to do the bedroom *tomorrow*. I don't care if it *is* Saturday. This is an *emergency*." As an afterthought, she added, "This is Hope. Call me *first thing* in the morning."

And now she had to get through an evening? With all these things on her mind, she had to put up a good front and go to a party?

Yes, that was exactly what she had to do. Her spine a

column of steel, she marched out into the living room wearing her warmest evening coat—the paisley one with the fake fur lining—and her best and most professional smile.

She found Sam on the sofa, looking as though he'd collapsed there, but of course he got right up and put his overcoat back on, and soon everything was back to normal, as though they hadn't had the most bizarre conversation ever held between two otherwise conservative human beings.

HE'D DONE IT. He didn't know how, but he'd done it.

The whole evening had felt different. Knowing that tomorrow night Hope's silken body would slide against his, that he would bury himself and his frustrations and his anxieties in her, sent a dart of tension through every word, every glance, every touch. When her hand crept around his elbow, he could feel the heat through all the layers of fabric that went into a penguin suit. Tonight, when she stood close to him, her breast brushed his arm and he took it as a promise, not an accident.

He hadn't dared to kiss her good-night. It would only have made the next twenty-four hours seem longer. She hadn't been far from his mind since their first meeting, and now, at long last, she was going to be his.

Sam shook his head, laughed a little at himself. Not Hope herself, sex with Hope, that's all that was on his mind. Not even "sex with Hope." Just sex. Pure carnal lust, about to be satisfied.

His inner smile faded. Wasn't that all he was thinking about?

Once again he was plagued by multisensory images—Hope laughing, her full, sexy mouth twisting in a teasing grimace, Hope's curtain of copper hair moving while she charmed a colleague of his or hers with her conversation, Hope's slim, energetic body beneath her simple, elegant clothes, a body bursting to get out, the body that would lie beside his tomorrow night, and under his, and on top of his...

This was Hope he was thinking about, not merely sex. Sam had a sudden feeling he was in deep trouble. He groaned.

"Don't complain to me about the traffic, buddy," the cab driver snarled. "It's Friday night, *knowwhatImean?* It's the holidays. Hell, it's Nyork. So chill. I'm doin' the best I can. You guys, always in a hurry, always kvetching..."

"YOU SAID FIRST THING. This is first thing."

Hope winced, held the receiver away from her vibrating ear and squinted at her watch. "I didn't mean six in the morning."

"Good thing I woke you up." Maybelle sounded cheery enough to earn Hope's hatred. "We've got work to do, hon. How long do we have to get the Ch'i flowing in your bedroom."

She didn't need any help with flowing. Pipe was her life. All she wanted was a more attractive bedroom. "Until seven tonight."

Maybelle's screech deafened her, but it also thoroughly awakened her. "Well, pull yourself together, sugah, and look for me to be there around nine."

"Why so long?" Hope had an uncontrollable desire to pipe some water onto the woman.

"Because I've gotta call folks, load stuff up. Well, 'bye, hon. Now you have some coffee and I mean *real* coffee before I get there because I can't do a *thang* for your life if your mood don't improve."

"I don't need any help with my life. I need help with my bed—"

But Maybelle had hung up.

Snarling softly, Hope got up from the sofa and began to fold her bedding. She didn't want Maybelle to know she'd been sleeping on the sofa. She didn't want Maybelle to know why she couldn't sleep on the sofa tonight. Well, she might sleep there, later on, after...after...

Coffee. Definitely. Lots of it.

"WE'RE HERE to move the bed."

The speaker was the most beautiful man Hope had ever had the pleasure of welcoming into her home on a frosty December Saturday, with the exception of his companion, who was marginally more beautiful. She couldn't feel the chemistry the way she did with Sam, but another woman would. They were virtually irresistible. And she was a woman with two unmarried sisters. She had to make a point of getting these guys' cards before they left.

But her matchmaking instinct would have to wait. "What do you mean, move the bed? Where's Maybelle?"

"She's guarding the truck until we get back." Adonis One smiled at her, revealing stunning white teeth. Then the two of them marched into her bedroom and flung off leather jackets to reveal black tank tops accessorized by salon tans and bulging muscles.

Hope scurried after them. "But how do you know where to, I mean, what's the purpose of moving the..."

Adonis Two whipped a screwdriver out of the tool

kit he wore on his belt and began to dismantle her bed frame, which was a fetching white wrought iron fantasy. "So feminine," the furniture salesman had said. Adonis One deftly ripped open the long box he'd been carrying under one massive arm and produced a plain steel frame, which he set up directly in front of the louvered doors that hid her bathroom and closet.

"We can't put the bed over there," Hope babbled as Adonis One finished up and sauntered into the living room. "How will I get to the bathroom? Somersault backward?"

"Ready to help with this?" Adonis Two called out.

He gripped one side of the box spring and mattress, while Adonis One reappeared to man the other side. Without visible effort they lifted the entire assemblage and started across the room with it.

"Uh-oh, Dickie, dust bunnies," Two said, looking over Dickie's shoulder.

"We'll get 'em later," Dickie said reassuringly.

As the bed settled into place on the frame, Hope heard an unfamiliar ringing sound. Dickie detached a phone from his studded leather belt. "Going fine, yes, ma'am," he said. "Be down in a minute."

"Is that Maybelle?"

Dickie nodded. Hope snatched the phone from his hand.

"What's happening here?" she quavered. "They've messed up my whole bedroom—" her eyes widened "—and where are they going with my *bed*?"

She began to chase Dickie and friend, the phone at her ear, but they were too fast for her.

"I was mighty lucky to get them boys on such short notice," Maybelle said. "Aren't they cute? Did you ever in your life see buns any better'n they've got?"

"They have very nice buns, yes," Hope snapped. The door of the next apartment opened. Her neighbor looked out and scowled at her as he scooped up his newspaper. She hadn't realized she was out in the hall yelling about men's buns. She darted back inside and slammed the door. "Now tell them to get those buns back here in my bed. I mean *with* my bed."

"Oh, hon, you don't want that bed," Maybelle said with sudden authority. "I'll explain it all to you someday when we've got the time for it. 'Bye."

Hope didn't have long to simmer. Maybelle, in pressed light blue jeans and a sparkling white shirt under a cloud-like white down coat, bustled in with Dickie. Between them they carried a large crate.

"Don't worry," Maybelle said breezily, although Hope hadn't offered any help, "it's not heavy."

When the two of them vanished into the bedroom together and began to make ripping noises, Hope backed quietly toward her big square glass coffee table, lowered herself to perch on it for a healing moment and sat down hard on the floor.

"Where is my coffee table?" she yelled, scrambling back onto her feet.

The ripping noises ceased. "It's..." Dickie began.

"I see it." The top was resting against the wall with the square marble base beside it. "What is it doing there?"

"Dickie's going to take it down to the truck in a while," Maybelle said.

"But *why*?"

She heard murmurs from the bedroom, and then Maybelle appeared in the doorway. "Hon," she began predictably, "we gotta get rid of your sharp edges."

"Maybelle," Hope said, struggling for patience.

"You're here to work on my bedroom, not my personality."

Maybelle's eyes, bluebonnet blue and alive with energy, opened wide. "Oh, you're not the one with the sharp edges. You're sweet as pie. It's your furniture's got the sharp edges."

She cast a nervous glance behind her into the bedroom. "Look, sugarpie, we don't got time for a tewtoryul in feng shui, but all it is, really, is fixing up what's in your home so you feel comfortable living there. Now you got other things to worry about before your gentleman friend gets here tonight. You put your mind on feedin' him and lookin' purty. I'll handle the rest."

"How do you know I'm expecting a gentleman friend?" Hope was suddenly all too aware of her baggy gray sweatsuit, her hair up in a ponytail, her scruffy aerobic shoes—and her empty larder.

"I been around some," Maybelle said succinctly. An annoyed exclamation came from the bedroom. She scurried away. Hope flung her hands up in the air, grabbed her handbag and coat and left to go shopping.

On the way out of the building, she encountered two illegally parked vehicles, a pickup truck, powder-blue with blue checked curtains tied back at each window, and a massive Cadillac, also powder-blue. Adonis Two lounged gracefully against the Cadillac.

It was a toss-up as to which vehicle Maybelle drove.

FEELING DAZED, Hope wandered among the soft chairs, kidney-shaped wood coffee table and squiggly side tables that seemed to fill her living room so comfortably. She had to admit it felt better. Warmer. More welcoming. A small round dining table with four upholstered chairs was another new addition. She felt serene enough to ignore the calculator in her head and the length of the strip of paper it was spitting out.

"Guess we're ready to show you what we did in here."

Hope moved reluctantly toward the bedroom to the rhythm of Maybelle's nonstop chatter. "Course, we had to get rid of that bed. Person could stick himself on all them iron vines. Besides, it squeaked. This frame? Industrial-strength. Won't squeak."

Hope paused, distracted by the notion of making beds squeak, then forced herself into the bedroom. "Oh, my," she said. "Oh, my goodness."

The bed was standing away from the closet and bathroom doors, but they'd attached a soft, padded thing behind it that surrounded it like arms, with round night tables tucked into the outer curves. It was covered in a faded flower print which matched the comforter. There were new linens, an ivy print in white and soft green. There were lamps on the night tables, tall, graceful ones with pink shades.

"It's so pretty," she murmured. "I guess I was expecting something...plainer."

"I wanted you to feel like you was in a flower garden," Maybelle said. Her strident voice was softer, too. "You seemed to like vines and flowers, so I gave you vines and flowers, friendlier ones."

There was a moment's silence before Hope said, "Where's the electricity coming from? For the lamps."

"Oh, for heaven's sake." Maybelle folded her arms across her thin chest and glared at Hope. "I'm not sure, but you may be hopeless, no pun intended. If you really have to know, Kevin ran the wire to over here under the bed."

"I'm sorry," Hope said, drooping. "I can't help being practical."

"Then let's get practical," Maybelle said. "Do you really want to lie in this bed—" she paused significantly "—with your family starin' at you from the dresser?"

Hope had a sudden image of herself in that leafy bower of a bed with Sam, the sweet faces of her parents looking at her, Faith and Charity sending her mischievous smiles. "No," she said decisively.

"Good. Candles'll be better." Maybelle whipped open a bag and placed a group of five candles, each a different color, on a tray on the dresser. "You two visit while I put another set in the living room."

She clicked out of the room. She was wearing white high-heeled boots, Hope noticed, to match her coat. Dickie stacked up the photographs, handed them to Hope and energetically dusted the top of the dresser with the cloth he'd hung over his muscled shoulder.

He stood back to admire his work. "We hung a wind chime in front of the heating duct in the kitchen, too. To help romanticize the place. That was my idea," he said, ducking his head modestly.

"I like wind chimes," Hope said. "Brass ones, anyway. They remind me of pipe." She glanced down at the photographs in her arms. "I just love this picture of my sisters," she said, and thrust it out to show him.

"Cute chicks," he said warmly.

"Aren't they?" She paused only briefly. "Dickie, are you and Kevin married?"

"Not yet," Dickie said. "We'll get married when the law changes, though. I was all for moving to Vermont where you can have a civil ceremony, but Kevvie says we'd better hang around New York. He's sure we're going to break into show biz any day now."

"Oh," Hope said. "Then I guess you wouldn't be interested in... No, of course you wouldn't."

Maybelle swooped down on them and added a sixth candle, another deep, rosy red one, to the group. "You need more fire in your life," she said inscrutably. "Dickie, run out to the truck and get them bamboo flutes. We gotta do something about that beam up there." She turned to Hope. "Beams can make you feel like the world's weighing you down. Some flutes will lift the weight up, up and away."

"Get that old *Ch'i* flowing, so to speak," Hope murmured. She gazed thoughtfully at the beam above them. "Don't bother going back to the truck, Dickie. I've got just the thing."

When they'd left, Hope gazed for a moment at the bed. Tentatively she sat on it, then lay down on it, then let herself sink more deeply into it.

It felt like being in the arms of the Jolly Green Giant.

ANTICIPATION had driven her body out of control. Just the buzz of the house phone, the doorman telling her he'd arrived, was enough to send a wave of heat coursing through her, to dry her mouth as the moisture fled toward those secret, hidden parts that wanted Sam, more of Sam, all of Sam. Her fantasies were no longer locked into her dreams; they'd tortured her every aching moment of the day.

She mustn't let him know what he did to her. It would end his trust in her as the perfect companion, the woman who had promised of her own free will that she would never ask anything of him emotionally.

Okay, so she wouldn't ask. She'd beg.

Hope mentally knocked herself in the head with a hammer. She wasn't this nervous before the Number 12867 presentation. She wasn't this nervous when she gave the valedictory address at her college graduation. She was almost but not quite this nervous the time their parents had put Faith and her in charge of Charity while they worked on the income tax, and Charity had climbed up on the roof of the garage and announced that she was Peter Pan and intended to fly through their bedroom window. But that was a long time ago, and this was *now*.

The trick would be to act casual, behave as though what was about to occur this evening was as commonplace for her as it was for Sam. In short, to disguise her nervousness by seeming to be even calmer than usual, which was hard to do when you were quaking inside, when you felt hot and cold all over by turns, when the tinkling of the wind chimes, supposedly a soothing influence, came across like the clanging of cymbals.

"Ah-a-ah!" Hope said, her heels lifting off the floor at the next sound she heard. The buzzer. Sam had arrived.

"Send him up," she told the doorman.

She had just enough time to take a look at herself in the mirror. She'd decided to wear a black-velvet jumpsuit without much under it and flat velvet slippers. At-home casual, not provocative, but not nunlike either. No jewelry, a little makeup, maybe she should change into something that could be removed by increments, but there wasn't time to change, she had to go with it, because at that moment the doorbell chimed.

She gave the plate-glass windows one last look, thinking if it weren't so cold she might jump, then opened the door.

As usual, the sight of him took her breath away. His eyes shone crystalline blue above his casual white sweater, black slacks and a charcoal-gray overcoat. More than that, it was an unusual treat to find a man standing at her door with one arm wrapped around a gigantic bouquet of lush island flowers, man-eating flowers in a profusion of rosy-red and cream, and the other wrapped around a large white poinsettia.

"Aloha and Merry Christmas," he said. "Guess which one is from me."

She thought he sounded a little cool for a man who was keeping an appointment for a night of passionate sport. "I'd be afraid to guess." She slid the bouquet from his grasp, staggering under its weight. "They're so—different. And both quite lovely," she added quickly.

He slid his briefcase—of course he'd bring his brief-case—off his shoulder, let it settle gently into the clos-est *fauteuil* and nodded at the bouquet. "That was downstairs and I volunteered to deliver it. I brought the Christmas spirit." He glanced down at the poinset-tia. "Where do you want it?"

She was right. He was cool.

"Let me think." She struggled over to her new coffee table with the bouquet and set it down, then scanned the room. "Let's put it there, right under the windows, so it's the first thing you see when you come into the room. Oh, Sam, it's beautiful."

"Should I leave while you read the card?"

"The card that came with the bouquet? No, of course not," she said. It appeared that a bouquet from heaven knew whom was about to destroy the evening. She vented her frustration on the card as she ripped it out of the envelope.

It began, "Hon..." She looked up and smiled, not needing to read any further. "It's from my decorator," she said. "She's been doing a few little things to the apartment. She's an—unusual person. Just like her to send flowers."

"I noticed some changes here and there," Sam said. At last he seemed to be warming up.

"I think these are ginger blossoms," Hope said, looking at the fat, fleshy flowers. A few morning glory-type flowers floated down from the edges of the bouquet. "I don't know what these are." She returned her attention to the card and read it aloud.

"She says, 'Hon, you have yourself a nice weekend.'" Hope paused, wishing she hadn't started. "'I made the man put in some passion flowers.'"

She halted completely as the telltale heat climbed her face. "'He said they wouldn't last. I said what the heck,'" Hope mumbled. "Signed 'Maybelle and the boys.'"

"Who are 'the boys'?"

Hope gazed at the man standing across the room, filling it with his aura of power, maleness and the delicious scent of cold air. All of a sudden she felt that everything would be fine. She lifted an eyebrow. "They are two of the most gorgeous men I've ever had the pleasure of meeting," she said, and sighed theatrically. "They spent most of the day in my bedroom without giving me a tumble."

She moved toward him, relishing the darkening uncertainty in his eyes, and cocked her head to one side. "On the other hand, one look at you, Sam Sharkey, could have done some serious damage to their relationship. With each other."

For a moment he gazed at her in silence. Then, "Let's

start over," he said abruptly. He reached down, swept up the poinsettia effortlessly and strode to the door.

"Sam, wait, don't—" Hope watched helplessly as the door closed behind him. As a terrible coldness swept through her, she saw he'd left his briefcase. "Sam!" she called again, just as the doorbell chimed. One sluggish step at a time, she moved toward the sound, then cautiously opened the door.

"Merry Christmas," Sam said. His voice was low and husky. He slid through the doorway, reached out, cupped her chin and brushed her mouth with his.

"Sam, you shouldn't have," she whispered.

He set the plant down on the floor and folded both arms around her, pulling her to him, tucking her under his overcoat, tight up against the softness of his sweater, the hardness of his chest.

His kisses feathered against one corner of her mouth, then the other. Sudden warmth drove away the cold, the heat and moisture between her thighs sending delicious rivulets of aching pleasure into her stomach, her breasts, out to her trembling fingertips.

His mouth was warm, too, and unbelievably soft as it slid across her cheek to her ear. She shuddered when his tongue tipped her earlobe, flicked into the shell. "Want to go out to dinner?" he murmured. "Someplace close?" The hot sweetness of his breath blew gently into her hair.

"Let's just stay here," Hope whispered. "I have lots of—"

His mouth took hers, stifling her words, driving every thought from her mind except her final admission of a desperate need, not merely for a man, but for this man.

7

FIRST, THERE HE WAS, big-time lawyer Sam Sharkey, acting like a jealous adolescent. Then the relief of knowing another man wasn't pursuing her, a man who might meet her needs better than he ever could, had turned him into an adolescent with a libido running amok. He had to kiss her, just had to, there was no arguing with himself, and the second he touched her he was a dead man.

He was too hungry for her to hide it. Her mouth, God help him, was even fuller, softer, more pliable than he'd remembered. His mouth slipped and slid over her glossy lipstick in a way that was orgiastic.

At the first signal from her that felt like a yes he parted her lips, slipping his tongue into her mouth, searching for the honey-sweetness he knew was hidden there for him alone to find. And she gave it to him, tangled her tongue with his, let him feel her own need. It rocked him to his very center, the way she felt against him as he gathered her closer. Hot and hard for her, nearly out of control, he'd lost interest in everything but taking possession of her.

His hands spread out over her back, luxuriating in the feel of her delicate bones under black velvet. She was small and fine, but so alive, so full of energy, he knew she would move under him, engage in the battle of two forces moving toward the same victory, and they would win gloriously.

For a moment he gave in to the fantasy that it would happen in one seamless sweep of time, that somehow all the steps would be behind them, their clothes would miraculously evaporate from their heated bodies and he would take her there, leaning against the door, empty both of them into the yawning vessel of their desperation.

But he couldn't let it seem like an act of desperation. It was, but not for the reasons she might imagine.

He had to slow down, slow down... *Sam*, he said to himself, *you've used up all your adolescent points for this calendar evening.*

If he didn't slow down, he was going to scare her, and then it would be all over. Putting it that way finally got the attention of the brainless parts of his body.

He eased away, letting his mouth linger on hers until the last second because he just couldn't help himself, and he almost lost it again when he sensed her own reluctance to let go. "That's a better beginning," he said. It was hard to talk. His throat had closed up. All his systems had shut down but one, and the less time he spent thinking about that one the better. "I know where we want this."

Hope was in a state of floating bliss. She registered his voice—low, rich and deep, it seemed to vibrate inside her, a kiss in itself—but had a hard time grasping the meaning of his words. *Anywhere's fine*, she thought dreamily. *In bed would be the most...* Oh. He meant the poinsettia.

He slipped his arms out of his overcoat and let it fall onto the *fauteuil* before he took the poinsettia to its spot under the windows, then stepped back as if he were admiring it. "What do you think?"

Blood rushed to the hot, damp apex of her thighs with an intensity that almost bent her double. *I think you're gorgeous. You have better buns than Dickie and Kevin, and I love the way your shoulders move when you walk. And even more than your looks I love your touch, your mouth, your hands, your arms, your—* "Looks great," she said, then cleared her throat. "Just right. We needed a little Christmas spirit around here."

He turned to her. His heavy-lidded eyes and come-fly-with-me smile jolted her into a sudden flurry of hostessing.

"I'll just put things out on the coffee table, okay? We can eat and talk and... Would you open the wine? White and red. In case one of us wants one or the other."

While she listened to herself prattle on incoherently she fluttered in and out of the kitchen, bringing out an array of specialty-store takeout food that in one of her saner moments, if she survived to see another one, she'd call "indecisive." Chinese ribs. Grilled baby lamb chops. Shrimp Remoulade. A platter of French cheeses with a thinly sliced baguette. Pasta salad. Tabbouleh. Greek salad redolent with feta cheese. Calamari salad.

She ran out of serving dishes. She'd bring the rest out if Sam still looked hungry. Then dessert. Many, many desserts. She'd had to take a taxi home from Zabars. It was only five blocks away.

Sam looked hungry. But she wasn't sure it was food he wanted, and she knew it wasn't what *she* wanted. She hoped he wouldn't see the things she'd bought for breakfast.

THE WIND CHIMES shimmered musically. Rachmaninoff's First Piano Concerto, turned down low, created an old-movie ambiance. Which old movie Hope couldn't remember, but it had seemed right at the time she was setting the stage. Outside, the snow fell relentlessly, hushing the sounds of the city.

On the sofa beside her, his knee brushing hers with an intimacy they'd shied away from before, Sam licked the last crumb of lemon tart out of the corner of his mouth. Hope followed the path of his tongue, remembering the way it had felt against hers, shivering with anticipation for what was surely to come.

It seemed clear to her that they'd done about all the postponing they could. It was time for the main event.

She could tell Sam thought so, too. He reached out for her hand, took it, turned it over, then gently raised it to his lips. "Tastes like raspberries," he said as he trailed his tongue over the tip of her index finger.

The caress sent a shiver through Hope. "Maybe you'd like a—"

"Another taste of you," Sam said. "That's all I want." He drew her closer. "If your fingertip tastes like raspberries, the odds are your mouth tastes like—"

"Wait," Hope said, scooting back.

"Right. We ought to clean up first."

Clean up? Cleaning up was the last thing on her mind.

"Do you have a tray?"

"A tray? I think so." Delighted to have a reprieve, she scurried into the kitchen, found a tray and scurried back. It took Sam about three minutes to load the contents of the coffee table onto the tray and carry it into the kitchen, locate the matching set of refrigerator storage containers with the blue tops she hadn't seen since she moved in, dump the leftovers into them, rinse the dishes and put them in the dishwasher.

"There," he said, "all done."

Maybe it hadn't taken just three minutes. All Hope knew was that he finished way too soon for her peace of mind.

"There's just a drop of the red wine left," he said next. "We'll share it."

"Wouldn't you like some coffee?" Hope asked. Hopefully.

"No."

The gaze he leveled at her told her in no uncertain terms what he wanted. But he sounded gentle when he said, "If you've changed your mind, if this is too much for you, just say so." He stroked her cheek, down under her chin, his thumb grazing her throat.

She felt the pulse beating there, beating hard. "No, no," she breathed. "I'm fine. It's fine. We're fine. I mean, we have a deal."

He smiled. In one effortless move he lifted her onto the kitchen counter, pushed her knees apart and moved between them. Cupping her startled face in his hands, he said, "Forget the deal. I'm not going to hold you to it if you regret making it."

As soon as his hands touched her kneecaps the waves of heat had begun to spread up her thighs. She tightened them against his waist, instinctively seeking the pressure of him against her, frustrated when it didn't quite work, their bodies didn't quite meet in the spot where she had gotten desperate for them to meet. "I don't." A husky croak was the best she could manage. "I don't regret it."

But she did have something important to say. "There are a couple of things we should bring right out in the open, I guess. We, ah," she hesitated a moment, "we will use, um, protection?" She made it into a question. She'd bought a box of three condoms and had stashed them in the drawer of her new night table.

"Well, sure." Sam said. He left her sitting on the counter while he brought his briefcase in from the living room. "Amazing," he said as he burrowed into it, tossing out a dopp kit, an undershirt, a sweater, "what you can get in a briefcase when you leave the laptop at home. Here we are." He brought out a box.

Hope drew in a sharp breath. *His* box of condoms was enormous. She did some quick mental calculations. If her box was sufficient for a one-night stand, then his box could handle a lengthy, flaming affair.

He must have read her thoughts. Or maybe just read the look on her face. "The big box was more economical than the small box."

"Oh, yes, of course," she murmured. Unless you counted the opportunity cost, what you could earn by investing the difference between the cost of her box and the cost of his. Hope shook her head a little in a desperate effort to shut off the left side of her brain.

"And look." He pointed to the message on the bottom of the box. "'Most effective if used before July, 2005.' I'd say we're safe, wouldn't you?"

Safe from pregnancy, maybe, but Hope didn't feel the least bit safe right now. His energy and enthusiasm were terrifying. The size of him was terrifying. The cheerful way he'd devoured a huge dinner, while she sat there having death-row thoughts, was terrifying. She was ready for darkness, nudity and a quick closure to this whole hazardous undertaking.

She had come to the conclusion that her life would have run more smoothly, been less challenging, if she'd never met Sam Sharkey. It was, however, a little late for that.

"Quite safe," she lied, "and that's good." She ripped her attention away from The Box to gaze at him earnestly. "Because it's important for us not to be nervous."

He put the box aside and resumed his position between her thighs, his face close enough to hers to turn the conversation into a kiss at any moment. "I'm not nervous. Are you?"

"Oh, heavens, no," she said, feeling the lies grow easier with practice. "And it wouldn't matter anyway. Not for me."

He stared at her, his eyes sending pinpricks of sparkle into her very soul. "Not for you. Just for me."

"Right. Because when a man gets nervous, it can affect the expansion and contraction of his, um, coupling gear."

She felt the involuntary jerk of his body, his withdrawal, putting an extra inch of space between them. "Coupling gear. Coupling gear?" Then felt him relax, felt the warmth as he leaned closer to her, his mouth moving toward hers. "Oh, Hope," he said, strangling the soft laughter in his voice. "You've been in pipe too long."

His kiss brushed her lips, then brushed them again on the wake of his sigh. "Don't be afraid," he whispered. "This is going to be fun."

His hands cupped her face, and his thumbs gently massaged her earlobes as he continued his soft, whispery kisses. For a moment she let herself flow along with the thrumming sensation from his light caresses. They felt sweet, delicious and not at all frightening. Pure pleasure.

PLAY BANGO!

AND GET THREE FREE GIFTS

It looks like BINGO, it plays like BINGO but it's FREE

HOW TO PLAY:

1. With a coin, scratch the Caller Card to reveal your 5 lucky numbers and see that they match your Bango Card. Then check the claim chart to discover what we have for you — 2 FREE BOOKS and a FREE GIFT — ALL YOURS, ALL FREE!

2. Send back the Bango card and you'll receive two brand-new Harlequin Temptation® novels. These books have a cover price of $3.99 each in the U.S. and $4.50 each in Canada, but they are yours to keep absolutely free.

3. There's no catch. You're under no obligation to buy anything. We charge nothing — ZERO — for your first shipment. And you don't have to make any minimum number of purchases — not even one!

4. The fact is, thousands of readers enjoy receiving our books by mail from the Harlequin Reader Service®. They enjoy the convenience of home delivery…they like getting the best new novels at discount prices, BEFORE they're available in stores…and they love their *Heart to Heart* subscriber newsletter featuring author news, horoscopes, recipes, book reviews and much more!

5. We hope that after receiving your free books you'll want to remain a subscriber. But the choice is yours — to continue or cancel, any time at all! So why not take us up on our invitation, with no risk of any kind. You'll be glad you did!

YOURS FREE!

This exciting mystery gift is yours free when you play BANGO!

It's fun, and we're giving away
FREE GIFTS
to all players!

PLAY BANGO!

SCRATCH HERE! →

CALLER CARD

YES! Please send me the 2 free books and the gift for which I qualify! I understand that I am under no obligation to purchase any books as explained on the back of this card.

YOUR CARD ↘

BANGO

38	9	44	10	38
92	7	5	27	14
2	51	FREE	91	67
75	3	12	20	13
6	15	26	50	31

CLAIM CHART!

Match 5 numbers	2 FREE BOOKS & A MYSTERY GIFT
Match 4 numbers	2 FREE BOOKS
Match 3 numbers	1 FREE BOOK

342 HDL DFUS

(H-T-OS-12/01)
142 HDL DFUR

NAME _____ (PLEASE PRINT CLEARLY)

ADDRESS _____

APT.# _____ CITY _____

STATE/PROV. _____ ZIP/POSTAL CODE _____

Offer limited to one per household and not valid to current Harlequin Temptation® subscribers. All orders subject to approval.

His mouth hovered over hers for a second, and then his kiss deepened. His fingers threaded through her hair as his hands found their way to her neck, her shoulderblades, until his arms closed around her. Pure pleasure gave way to something more demanding as she returned the kiss.

His arms tightened around her waist and he lifted her off the counter, sliding her down his body with a sensuous slowness, letting her feel his arousal until at last he held her just where she'd wanted to be, her breasts tight against his chest, his hardness against her heat. She heard his breath quicken, felt the moan rise in her own throat.

His quiet, persuasive assault seemed to last for hours. She floated on a cloud of escalating desire. A storm was building up inside that cloud. She could feel it in the pounding of her heart, the shortness of her breath, the waves of euphoria that swept over her.

The change in tempo wasn't sudden, but it was definite. His mouth felt harder against hers. His tongue explored more deeply, exciting her to play against him, thrust hers against his. His hands cupped her buttocks, caressing them through the velvet, through the silk of her panties, molding her body ever more closely to his.

She was aware that he was moving them toward the bedroom, engaging her in an enticing dance she wished would last forever. They were almost there, almost there. He pushed the bedroom door open with his elbow. Through half-closed eyes she saw the candles burning, just as she'd left them, waiting for this moment.

It was her turn to lead now. She reached out with her hand toward the bed—and lurched suddenly to one side.

He caught her, held her tighter. She could feel the hard pounding of his heart against her breasts. His words rasped against her ear. "What's wrong? You okay?"

"I can't," she gasped, "I can't..."

"Hope." It came out as a groan. "Can't what? Can't..."

"I can't find the bed."

He stood absolutely still for a second, then suddenly swept her off her feet and cradled her in his arms.

"I'll find it, don't you worry. Like an explorer in uncharted territory."

Level with the foot of the bed he paused again. "You are an amazing woman, Hope Sumner." He took a step forward. "You have hair like copper and eyes like emeralds." Another step. "You're smart, you're cute, you're funny." Step, step, step. "It makes me happy just to be with you." The last step. "And tonight you're mine."

He laid her gently on the flowered coverlet and slid down beside her.

When he put his hand, such a warm, strong, smooth hand, to her throat, trailing one finger down, she thought her heart might stop beating.

He unbuttoned the first satin button and then another. He trailed his finger across her skin, moving closer and closer to her breasts and finally sliding it down between them.

She moved restlessly against his touch and heard his breathing quicken. Then his lips were against her skin, just above her breasts, nudging the lace of her bra aside, moving hotly, inexorably downward.

Her nipples tingled, tightened. She moaned, raising her body to meet his kiss.

He slid his hands behind her to unfasten the strip of lace. It fell away and her breasts were open to him, open to his mouth, his fingertips, his tongue. He teased them, circling them until she wanted to pound her fists against his back out of pure frustration. She wanted more, so much more.

"I think you should stop doing that," she whispered, raking her fingernails across the back of his sweater, wanting to feel skin instead.

"Why?"

"Because it's making me crazy." She pulled his head away from her breasts and brought his mouth to hers, her fingers threaded through his hair, her body searching for his.

"That's the idea," he managed to say before he yielded to her, giving her the kiss she wanted and needed, hard and hot, and crushing her against the full length of his body.

More hardness, more heat. More than she could bear. She rolled over him, straddling him, hearing his gasp of surprise.

His hands gripped her buttocks to pull her hard against his erection, and at last she was where she'd longed to be. Almost. There was still one thing wrong with the picture. There was still too much between them.

Slowly she sat up, still straddling him, and gazed down at him. His eyes glittered with stars of their own in the flickering candlelight. She unbuttoned one more button, just to watch his eyes widen, then darken with increasing excitement. Another button, then another, until she reached the waist, then she slipped the velvet and lace off her shoulders and in her half-nakedness, gave him more of herself than she'd ever given another man.

He seemed awed by the sight of her as his hands came up to cup her breasts, to stroke them again, gently, then with increasing pressure. It was ecstasy, being touched like that. She leaned into his hands and rocked against him, seeking more of him against her, feeling the tremulous beginnings of something building inside her that was almost frightening in its intensity. When she groaned, he picked up her rhythm, moving with her, increasing her pleasure. Her eyes lost their focus. She felt more than saw the flickering candles, the shadows they made against the walls, the rapid bucking of his hips beneath her.

She was falling, falling into an abyss of aching delight. With a surprised cry she fell forward into his waiting arms.

And instantly moaned, "I'm sorry, I'm sorry. I don't know how that happened. I didn't mean to...it wasn't the way it was supposed to..."

He tipped her over onto the coverlet and smothered her words with his lips, then lifted himself just enough to say, "Oh, yes it was. That was so good. So good."

She slid her mouth out from under his. "Was it really. Was it okay for me to..." He was tugging her jumpsuit over her hips, down her thighs, and she tried to help him, only managing to get completely in his way.

"Not just okay." He pulled the jumpsuit away, tossed it away into some distant corner of the room and quieted, gazing at her body, now naked except for her black lace bikini panties. "It's...it's..."

She'd rendered him speechless. At last he got his voice going again, and his hands.

"It's essential." He was breathing hard as he hooked his thumbs into the elastic of the panties and guided them in the same direction he'd sent the jumpsuit. "Call me crazy, but I just...can't...feel a thing..."

He tossed the panties. "...until I know you've had almost all you can stand at one time..."

He sat up, pulled his sweater over his head and disposed of it in one swift gesture. "And we're nowhere close to that point..." He unzipped his slacks and seemed to snake himself out of them, then flung back the coverlet and nestled her into the bower of sheets where he lay beside her at last, as naked as she was, and at last he was silent.

His voice was silent. The rest of him spoke poems of desire. For a moment she drank in the beauty and the sheer power of him, the breadth of his shoulders, the vee of dark curls that fanned across his chest and dived below his narrow waist, the muscles of his legs, and most of all, the mute evidence of his need for her. Barely giving her time to explore him with her gaze, he buried his face between her thighs, unerringly found the spot where she still throbbed, felt swollen, and caressed it with the tip of his tongue.

She felt she was pretty close to the point that she couldn't take any more. She was lost, lost in a pool of animal instinct. She'd lost her ability to worry about his reaction to her—did he like the way she looked without clothes, was he having a good time? She could feel nothing but the currents that raged inside herself as his tongue dipped and darted, teased that tiny part of her that held the secret to her pleasure.

She was on the brink, welcoming the rising tide, when he began to move up her body, kissing and tasting her stomach, darting his tongue into her navel. She couldn't help the little cry that exploded from her.

He slid up and up, reaching her breasts, teasing them with his tongue in a circling dance before his mouth closed on one nipple, then the other.

Every move of his body sent a message to the lower half of her body, where that tiny part of her was making such urgent demands she could hardly concentrate on anything else. She nudged herself closer to him, fluttering her fingertips over his back, his shoulders, into the silk of his hair, then returning to sink her fingers into the crisp curls that tickled against her skin, finally searching for the one thing she wanted and at last finding it.

When her hand closed on the hot shaft he groaned, moved within the circlet she'd made around him. He felt so silky, so different from the rest of him. She looked at his face, his eyes half-closed, his dark hair making damp ringlets against his forehead, his mouth swollen, his lips parted, and felt an affection for him so strong, so sharp, that it frightened her.

"I want this. I want it now," she whispered, wishing again for an end to the sweet pain, wanting life to go back to normal.

"Not yet." He seemed to struggle to speak. "Not quite yet," as his fingertips slid back down to her womanly core to tease, torment and then to bury themselves in her.

She arched against him, feeling the wave coming again, threatening to wash over her and carry her away, concentrating on herself again, because she could think of nothing else but the sensation closing in on her. It happened all of a sudden, no time to think, no time to do anything but feel, to cry out from the intensity of the feeling because it was so much stronger than before, lifted her so much higher.

He held her tight against him until at last she fell limp against the sheets.

She opened her eyes. They were wet with tears. She held out her arms. "Now, please," she said. "Now you."

His gaze probed her as his hand stroked her face, smoothed away the moisture of tears and perspiration. His mouth moved over hers in the gentlest of kisses. She could feel the way he held himself back, even now.

SAM WAS THINKING that now was the time he should probably go home, tell her he'd changed his mind. Not that he'd pretend he didn't want her—no way he could do that with any credibility because his desire spoke for itself—but simply explain that he cared too much to follow through with the deal under false pretenses.

That he was in deep danger of falling in love with her was something he couldn't hide from himself any longer. Falling in love with a woman who couldn't possibly fit into his life plan. Couldn't hide it from himself, but he had to hide it from her.

Try explaining that to his body, though, now that he'd tasted her, touched her, given her pleasure and gotten pleasure from it himself.

Even her quick arousal, her cries of delight, couldn't hide her lack of experience. He'd found it touching, exhilarating, because everything she felt was real, not practiced. Tonight would mean something to her, more than it should, because he couldn't fit into her life plan, either. Two people as driven as they were needed support at home, not a comet flying off in another direction to come back to earth a hundred years later.

Try telling that to his body. Feeling a groan rise from deep inside him, he reached for the condoms he'd dumped on the bedside table, quickly covered himself with one and rolled her over until she was straddling him, sitting up, gazing down at him.

She touched him, her breath quickening, her eyes glittering like gems in the candlelight. She grasped the tip and edged herself closer. His thoughts moved further and further to the background. She'd said yes. What else mattered? She was an adult. He was an adult. Whatever happened, each of them was responsible.

She lowered herself over him, panting, aroused, wanting in a way he'd always dreamed of a woman wanting him. When he met the slight resistance he'd wondered about, even feared, he found the presence of mind to say, "Are you sure? Is this what you want?"

"Yes. Oh, please, yes," was all she said, and then it was done, he'd broken through her maidenhead, felt his own surprise and hers, and then he entered a world of fire and flood, heat flowing like lava through his veins.

He could feel her tears falling on his chest, but she seemed unaware of them as she rocked with him, lost in her own apparent pleasure and need. His breathing quickened as the pressure built up inside him. He fought it down, struggling to hold back, desperate with the need to let go, but wanting her to share it with him. He held back until her sharp cry sounded in the quiet room and she collapsed against his chest, and at last he succumbed, holding on to her for dear life.

When the storm had let up, he rolled her to his side, not letting go. "You okay?" he whispered. His voice was funny, didn't work very well.

"Oh, yes, very, very, very okay." She hesitated, then whispered brokenly, "And very glad to be a woman."

"I am, too," he rasped against her hair. "Glad you're a woman."

"You gave me so much before you took anything for yourself."

She couldn't imagine how much he'd taken for himself. "For a woman," he said, smiling in the darkness, "the pleasure is infinite. For a man..."

Even as he spoke he felt himself hardening, felt the need rising again, wondered if he would frighten her by giving in to it. "A man," he began again, "has to wait, oh, two or three minutes in between." And he gave up, gave in, reveling in her soft, surprised laughter as she pulled him tight against her.

IN THE MIDDLE of the night, she lay cuddled in his arms, dreamy and peaceful after yet another session of lovemaking, slow this time and infinitely satisfying. It was such an effort to move her head, but she did, rolling it up a little to gaze at him in the light from the candles that flickered from the dresser top.

She found him staring fixedly at the ceiling. "What's up there on the beam," he said. His voice was rough with sleepiness. "Those things with the ribbons on them."

"Pipe," Hope said. "Pieces of pipe."

"Oh." He yawned, snuggled her tightly to him and was soon asleep.

8

A LOW CRY of pain and a string of muttered not-quite-curses woke Hope up, not the dancing light that filled the room.

"Curtains, curtains," Sam moaned.

He was either dreaming it was "curtains" for one of his clients or pleading with her to pull the curtains. Which she couldn't do, because there weren't any.

"Do you want a mask?" she whispered.

Sam was lying flat on his back. He turned his head an inch, so that one deep blue eye squinted at her. When he squinted, his long lashes folded almost in half. She could tell she'd confused him.

She made circles around her eyes with her fingers. "You know, the kind they give you on the airplane so you can sleep."

"Oh. No, that's okay. I'm getting used to it," he said at last. His lashes struggled open.

"It must be late," Hope said. She carefully assumed the same position he was in, flat on her back and staring up, and they lay there in silence for a moment.

"I'd say eight o'clock."

"I've never slept until eight o'clock," Hope said. "If you slept late, you'd need curtains or shades in a room like this." The ceiling was an ever-changing pattern of triangles as the sun hit the icicles that hung outside the windows. The effect was rather pretty. She couldn't help herself. She inched a millimeter closer to Sam's big warm body.

"I've never slept until eight o'clock, either," Sam said. "Summer, though, I do sleep past four. That's when the sun comes up in July."

"I guess that's when I wake up in July," Hope said.

"Sometimes I spend weekends in the country," Sam said. "There it's birds."

Hope nodded. "This is a little high for birds."

"To warble at each other, anyway," Sam said. "I guess up here they just fly on by."

Sunlight danced on the beam, lit up the slanted lengths of copper pipe with their bows of rosy red ribbon. The telephone rang. Hope didn't move.

"Aren't you going to answer it?" Sam asked her.

"No."

"Don't you want to know who it is?"

"I know who it is. I can feel who it is. And I think it must be later than eight o'clock."

"Why?"

"Because if it's eight o'clock here," Hope said, "it's only five o'clock in California and seven o'clock in Chicago."

"That's what it would be, all right."

The ringing ended; a muted voice that had the staccato rhythm of Charity at her bossiest came from the office alcove as the answering machine picked up. Hope knew she only imagined that Sam inched a centimeter toward her as they lay there in silence, staring at the ceiling.

She'd just had the most important, most exciting night of her life. Even though every second of it thrilled through her as she lay there so quietly, it was something she simply couldn't talk about, not even to Sam, who'd made it happen. And never, never would she be able to share it in giggly girl-talk with her sisters.

He tilted his head just a bit, following her gaze to the beam. "Pipe's a phallic symbol, you know," he said.

"Is not," Hope said at once.

"Is too." He nodded. "All these years you've been substituting pipe for penises."

She half-rose, reached behind her and grabbed up a pillow. "I have not!" She raised the pillow over her head.

"Hey, don't yell at me. I'm not the one with pipe envy." Sam rolled smoothly off the bed just as she slammed the pillow into the spot where he'd been lying.

At the doorway to the bathroom, in all his naked masculine glory, not at all shy the morning after, he turned to give her a wicked smile. "Don't move," he said. "I'm going to brush my teeth and get fresh supplies, and then I'm coming back to relieve your need for pipe. Forever."

His sexy growl and the mention of fresh supplies were almost her undoing, but she was still mad about the pipe thing. "Wait just a minute," she told him. "This was supposed to be an emergency treatment, not a marathon." Besides, the longer he stood in the doorway, the longer she had to memorize the lines of his body, the swell of his muscles. All the details she'd hold in her heart for the rest of her life.

"But we might as well be thorough while I'm here," he said. "It's the only efficient way to go." He closed the bathroom door behind himself.

Hope leaped out of bed, found her robe and darted out of the bedroom and into the powder room. She kept a toothbrush there. He was right. When you already had the assembly line set up, you might as well do another run.

Pipe envy. For heaven's sake.

AT TWO THAT AFTERNOON, Sam sat up feeling purposeful. As he dusted off the crumbs of breakfast in bed—toasted corn muffins with butter and honey—and lunch in bed—warm Brie, French bread and grapes, he pondered the amazing effect the honey had had on the right side of his brain. Usually quiet and unobtrusive, it had suddenly sprung into action, arousing his creative powers to new heights—as well as other parts of him. It had been buckwheat honey, strong and potent. For the rest of his life its sharp, sweet tang would mingle with the sharp, sweet taste of Hope on his tongue.

"I know how we should spend the rest of the afternoon," he announced.

"So do I," Hope said. "Working."

"Getting you a Christmas tree," Sam said, ignoring the comment about working. He'd known that's what she'd say.

"I don't need a Christmas tree," Hope protested. "I've got a poinsettia. I'll put lights on it."

"Not the same," Sam said.

"I'll be going home for Christmas," she said, building her argument. "Every year Mom tries to recreate Macy's. It's all the holiday spirit I can handle."

Still he ignored her. Best way to deal with Hope, he'd figured out. "You've got room for it. It'll spruce things up."

"Puns, yet," Hope groused, but he noticed she was slipping out of bed and into a robe—why she kept putting on the robe he couldn't imagine—and looking lively. "Well, maybe just a little tree."

"Umm," he hummed noncommittally. "You take the first shower," he said. "I'll make a list of equipment we'll need. Or..." He eyed her contemplatively. "...we could shower together and make the list later."

Under the shower, Hope confronted the worst of all possibilities, that Sam had all the equipment she'd ever need—for the rest of her life.

Dusk was falling when Sam slipped generous tips to the two building porters who'd struggled a nine-foot blue spruce into the service elevator and at last deposited it on the floor of Hope's living room.

"I deserve at least a fiver myself," Hope complained, dropping several shopping bags to the floor with a thud.

"Careful with those ornaments," Sam said with a sharp glance up from the tree stand box he was ripping into.

"Are we in agreement about the lights?" Hope asked. "Because the lights were always my thing when I was a kid, and I can't stand it if they're not..."

"I can guess. Evenly spaced."

"I used a triangle."

"I bet the tinsel has to go on one strand at a time."

"I always dreamed of tinsel put on one strand at a time," Hope said mournfully, "but Faith was in charge of tinsel and Faith has a more...random approach to life. Charity, well, Charity got to do the ornaments, but Mom wouldn't let her stand on a ladder when she was little, so they were all at the bottom at first and as she grew, they moved up. It was a terrible-looking tree until Charity reached her full height," she finished up, feeling a strange longing to return to that terrible-looking tree. "She grew to be awfully tall. Her trees look great now."

"Do you have some old clothes to change into?" Sam asked her. "When we put the tree in the stand, things could get messy."

Hope took a look at the spruce needles, then glanced down at her emerald-green sweater. "Snaggy is what they could get. Okay, I'll change." She supposed it was time for Sam to see her in the baggy sweats she liked to slouch around the house in. It might put a lid on the warm, snuggly feelings that had been zinging between them all afternoon like a subtext to their practical discussion of lights per tree-foot and silver and gold versus red and green.

In the end she'd reminded him that a decision should go to the one with a conviction, and she had a conviction that silver balls, crystal icicles and tinsel— hung one strand at a time—were meant to decorate her tree. But then she'd added a couple of dozen inexpensive terracotta-rose ornaments to the mix. Maybelle had said she needed more fire in her life, and so far, Maybelle seemed to know what she was talking about.

Pulling her hair up into a careless, ratty-looking ponytail, Hope paused. Last night had been fire and flood, hardness and softness, darkness and light. Thinking about it created a heavy ache between her thighs, moistened her, made her breath come faster. Her lips parted. She snapped them shut.

So she and Sam had yin and yang. So what? She briskly fastened the ponytail with a pink elastic band and went out to help with the tree-raising.

"IF I MOVE that one to the left," Sam said, "it's going to be too close to the one there at the back."

"So we'll have to move the one there at the back."

"Which will jam it right up against the one behind it."

"Are we having our first fight?" Hope asked him, feeling a bit frosty about the whole enterprise.

"Of course not. We're attacking a problem together, as a team. We're having a discussion of possible solutions. I have one possible solution."

He started down the ladder, reaching for her, but Hope neatly evaded him. The sweats hadn't had their desired negative effect on the hormone-heavy air. They did feel soft and comfortable. She was just a little bit sore, although not sorry about it.

"*That* would not solve our problem," she informed him. "It would merely be a stopgap measure. I feel obligated to point out that if we'd used the triangle in the first place, we wouldn't be in this predicament."

"It's not a predicament. It's a Christmas tree." Sam came down the three-step ladder and regarded her for a moment. "Okay," he said, "we'll do it your way."

"Oh, good," Hope said. "I love getting my own way."

"Do you?" He moved closer.

She edged back. "A lot." She shimmied out of his embrace and went off in search of her trusty triangle.

She found it in the walk-in closet in a plastic container labeled "Tools." She'd never seen the container before. She stood in the center of the closet, transfixed, gazing at a home-magazine vision of life in perfect order.

Tubs on wheels were labeled, "Cleaning Supplies," or "Catalogs." More plastic containers of varying sizes with matching mint-green lids lined the shelves in alphabetical order—"Office Supplies," "Sewing Supplies," "Shoeshine Kit."

"You okay?" Sam moved up behind her. "Wow. It's like a store in here."

"Another contribution from the decorator," Hope said. "She has this *thing* about keeping possessions in order. Here's the triangle. Let's get going on those lights."

But still they gazed at the closet shelves.

"You actually have empty spaces," Sam said. "There. Between Candles and Dry Cleaning. You've got room for Coca-Cola and Diet Pepsi."

"Or cat food."

"You getting a cat?"

"Thinking about it."

Sam's gaze zoomed toward the largest of the containers that sat under the shelves. Hope was already blushing hotly when he read the label. "Pipe." His head swiveled. "You have a pipe collection."

"It's just pipe samples," Hope said, feeling cross about being embarrassed.

"The folks at Revlon cosmetics, let's say, get to take home free lipstick, and you get pipe."

"Well, yes."

"And you bring it home and save it."

"It helps to have samples here," she said stiffly. "I don't stop working when I leave the office."

"Sure," Sam said. "I should have known that. You have any Number 12867 in there?"

She eyed him suspiciously, but his expression was deadly serious. "The star of my collection," she said.

He nodded, seeming to be lost in thought. Then he edged closer. "It's sort of nice in here."

"Cozy," she agreed, still suspicious.

"A microcosm of what you wish your whole life could be."

"A *what?*"

"Don't play dumb with me, wench. You know what I mean. Don't you wish your life could be in order like this closet? Everything in its place? With a lid on it that stays closed until you have time for it?"

"And room for everything," Hope murmured, getting interested in the idea. "All the things a life should have. Some 'Office Supplies,' some 'Cleaning Supplies,' some..."

"*F* for Family and Friends," Sam said, standing very close behind her, "*P* for Passion."

She shivered a little as his arms closed around her. "*L* for Love, *M* for Marriage," he went on, "and there's room in *C* for Cat Food *and* Children."

The words stilled the air. Hope turned in his arms to gaze up at him. His face was a mystery, revealing nothing. She asked him, "You want all those things?"

"Someday. You?"

"Someday."

A sigh, or maybe it was just a deep breath, or maybe he was feeling the beginnings of claustrophobia, seemed to rise up through him. "I had some good news this week," he said. "Good and bad."

She waiting, knowing, somehow what he was about to say.

"The Magnolia Heights case is going to court. I'm in charge of it."

Her eyes widened and her heart began to pound. Too many thoughts fought for dominance—hot defense of her product, pride in Sam and glad feelings for him. And that frantic exchange of e-mails no one knew about, presumably, except her and the parties writing those messages.

"Phil as much as said it means I'm getting the partnership."

On this topic she had no conflict in her feelings. She put her arms around him and gave him a hard hug. "Oh, Sam, I'm so happy. I know what this means to you." She drew back to smile at him. "When will you know for sure?"

"About the partnership? The partners meet on December twenty-first. It'll be kind of a Christmas cliffhanger." He gave her a wry smile. "All part of seeing what kind of stuff we're made of. Can we handle the tension without cracking."

"Of course you can," Hope said firmly. "You'll be working too hard to think about anything but the case."

Including me. Was that what he was trying to tell her? That he wouldn't have time for her, that their deal would end after the holidays? That's all they'd contracted for, really. It was what she'd wanted when they made the deal. Why did it suddenly seem like such a bad idea?

She felt better when he relaxed a little. When he spoke, the mischief, the sparkle, the wickedness had returned to his voice. "That starts tomorrow," he said. "In the meantime, we have a tree to light."

It broke the mood, and she felt half-relieved, half-sorry. Halves again. Whatever could have happened to her focus? She'd get it back, by golly, or die trying.

"My triangle, sir," she said, saluting smartly. "The solution to our problem. You're going to thank me for this," she said as she marched out of the closet.

"THAT'S EVERYTHING but the star on top."

"How could I have forgotten the star?" Hope said. "I

accept full responsibility," she assured him. "I was head of the Ornaments Task Force, as I recall."

"A small detail and easily fixed," Sam said in a way that both agreed she was the accountable party and generously excused her lapse. "I've got a business lunch tomorrow in midtown. I'll buy a star on the way back to the office."

But Hope was eyeing the tree from a Palmer Pipe perspective. "If you do," she said, "keep the receipt. You can take it back if I think of an alternative."

"What time is it?" he said abruptly.

She glanced at her watch, realizing she hadn't looked at her watch since...

...since six-fifty-five the evening before when she waited for Sam. Since then, life had been timeless, without boundaries. Tomorrow was Monday, a return to the real world for Sam and for her. She didn't like the feeling that hit the pit of her stomach at the thought, which was odd, because she usually looked forward to Monday morning.

"Seven. Are you hungry? I've got tons of leftovers."

He tipped up her chin with one hand. "Truth time."

"Okay."

"If you want me to leave, we're at a good stopping place."

The words stumbled out of her. "Well, no, I..."

"I said be honest."

She gazed into his eyes. She didn't think she could stand it if he left. "No," she whispered, "I don't want you to leave, but if you have things to do, I under-stand."

"Of course I have things to do. I always have things to do. Now I have even more things to do. I just don't feel like doing them right this minute. I've got a lid on them."

She nodded.

"You have things to do, too," he said. She noticed the glint of amusement start up in his eyes. "It's Sunday night, the night, as I recall, to put on the masque."

And condition her hair and manicure and pedicure. She glanced at her fingernails. She'd shredded a couple of them on the tree and the others just looked...used. "It can wait."

He smiled, flashed white teeth at her and crystal glints from his eyes. "In that case, I'm going out to run a couple of errands."

"Well, okay, I..."

He could spring into action faster than anyone she'd ever known. "Put out the leftovers," he said, sliding his arms into his overcoat and wrapping his scarf around his neck. "I'll be back in forty-five minutes. Need anything while I'm out?"

She was no slowpoke herself. "Yes. If you just happen to run into a Styrofoam ball about—oh, about this big—and some of that fake gold-leaf paint, that would help."

He gazed at her for a long, slow minute. "Where would I run into them?"

"I'd try a drug store."

"Gotcha." A quick smile and he was gone.

Forty-five minutes. She had no time to waste. Into the dishwasher, out with the clean dishes from the night before. Into the refrigerator and out with the ribs, baby lamb chops, the Chinese chicken wings they still hadn't touched. Salads. Cheeses. Desserts.

Into the bathroom—nail file, polish remover, clear polish. Cuticles would have to wait. She put her supplies on the night table nearest the telephone and sat down on the bed. Cotton square in hand, she dialed.

"Hey!" said the familiar voice.

"Maybelle, it's me. Hope." She tipped the polish remover bottle over the cotton square and began to swipe at her fingernails.

"How you doing, hon?" Maybelle said.

"Fine. Thanks for the flowers. They're gorgeous."

"Did the passion flowers last?"

Hope smiled inside. "They're still hanging in there. Anyway," she hurried on, seeing dangerous territory ahead, "I wondered if you could come by Tuesday night and we could, well, finalize things." She tossed the cotton square into the wastebasket and picked up the file.

"Well, sure." Maybelle paused. "You sure you're okay?"

"Absolutely," she said, filing madly. Why she felt this sudden need to talk to Maybelle she couldn't imagine. How could Maybelle help her with the tangle she saw herself getting into?

Her thoughts went back to the tidy, organized closet. Everything with lids on it. Because Maybelle did more than decorate. She untangled people's lives.

Hope slapped clear polish on the nails of her right hand, the receiver tucked up under her chin. "So I'll see you Tuesday. We can discuss what else you'd like to do here. Maybe you could get my bill together between now and then."

A low cackle came from the receiver, but it wasn't an unkind sound. "Sure," Maybelle said. "Now you keep puttin' water in them flowers, hon, and they'll last forever."

"Even the passion flowers?" All her movements slowed.

Maybelle's voice softened. "Maybe not as long as the others, but plenty long enough."

After she hung up Hope sat on the bed for a moment, feeling thoughtful. Then, with one last stroke of polish to the little finger of her left hand, she scurried out of the bedroom, wiggling her fingertips in the air.

When Sam returned she'd covered the little round table in newspaper and had laid out several dozen pieces of slender pipe in varying lengths. She'd changed clothes, too, and was wearing a long purple velvet lounging dress. She was naked beneath it, which she hoped would come as a nice surprise to him when he discovered it.

He eyed her first, then the display set out on the table. Wordlessly he hauled a Styrofoam ball and a can of gold spray paint out of one of the bags he carried. "Why am I so sure that's going to be a star when you finish it?"

"E.S.P.?" Hope asked, smiling brightly at him.

IT WAS UNFORTUNATE that the telephone rang. It was even more unfortunate that she answered it.

"You can't do this to us, Hope," Faith said. She sounded tearful.

"Not return a call for hours and hours," Charity said, sounding officious.

"We called Mom and Dad and told them we thought you might be dead," Faith snuffled.

"You did not!" *My sisters,* she mouthed at Sam. She lifted her eyebrows to indicate her exasperation, then laid a shushing finger across her lips.

"We were about to," Charity assured her. After a

short silence, she said, "What's that I hear in the background?"

"Christmas carols," Hope muttered.

"'Joy to the World', Faith, I hear 'Joy to the World.'" Charity spoke in tones of wonder.

Sam trailed a finger across her cheek, then lifted a cup of eggnog to her lips. She wondered if her sisters could hear eggnog. "Well, it *is* the season," she informed them.

"But you've never sat around listening to Christmas carols before."

"Are we calling at a bad time?" Charity said suddenly.

They were psychic. They *could* hear eggnog. For all she knew, they could hear her breath quicken as Sam licked a drop of eggnog from the corner of her mouth and set down the cup to pull her back against him, into his arms. When he buried his mouth at her nape, she shivered with the delicious sensation.

"Well, it *is* my grooming night," she said. Her voice went up the scale and back down. Sam's low chuckle vibrated the full length of her spine. "Let's talk tomorrow."

After she'd hung up she just let herself sink back into his embrace. "I have an idea," he murmured into her hair.

She had little doubt what sort of idea he'd just had. Up tight against him, she discovered that parts of him other than his brain had their own ideas. "You're full of ideas this evening," she said. "What now?"

"This *is* your grooming night." As he mimicked her, his voice grew husky. "I'll help you with your grooming."

"What a lovely idea." She turned a little in his arms. "Where shall we start?"

"You choose. Toes or fingers." His tone was languid, his eyes heavy-lidded.

"I usually start by soaking my toes," she said, brushing some light kisses across his chin for punctuation. She gasped when she felt him spin her around, resting her head on one arm of the sofa and his own on the other. "Sam, what are you... Sam, I said *soaking* my toes, not..."

He'd pulled off her velvet slipper and taken her toe into his mouth, where he surrounded it with more velvet as he circled his tongue around it, sucked gently at it while he caressed the rest of her toes, her ankle, her calf. Fingers of flame leaped upward through her veins, stabbing at her core, dissolving her into a jelly of pure desire. His fingertips traveled up her calf, then retreated.

He drew her toe slowly out of his mouth to trace a path up and over each of the other toes, then down between them, up and down, with the tip of his tongue. She groaned, arching toward him. Her toes felt wonderful, but the rest of her felt deeply deprived. Her mouth felt swollen, her nipples were so taut and hard that her breasts ached, and the even harder ache between her thighs was growing in intensity, becoming more demanding.

She would have more of him. She had to. She dug her other foot down between his legs, inching forward, forcing them apart, feeling his jolt of response and hearing the animal sound in his throat as her foot finally reached its mark, resting fully against the length of his hardness.

She could feel him losing interest in her toes. His

eyelashes fluttered down to his cheeks, his breathing was labored.

"That's one foot," he murmured hoarsely, reaching for the one that was giving him such torture.

She gave it willingly, merely replacing it with the other. He began to move against her as he suckled the toes of the one foot and she wriggled the toes of the other against him.

It took more concentration than she could manage at the moment. The heaviness between her thighs had become more uncomfortable. She had to do something about it, she really had to. She had to get control of this situation and...

"This would be more fun," she panted, "if you were naked."

"How could it be any more fun?" He could barely speak. His caresses were becoming more random as his own need grew, his fingers stroking the skin of her thigh, coming closer to her heat.

"I'll show you." She arched forward and grasped at his belt buckle, his zipper. He abandoned his attack on her toes to help, letting her slide his clothes away from him and toss them on the floor. She pulled his sweater over his head, cursing when it tangled, trapping him.

Taking advantage of the opportunity she darted quickly into the bedroom and returned, where she found Sam just where she wanted him, sitting up on the sofa, naked and struggling out of the wrists of the sweater.

She pulled one wrist free and held it tightly as she grasped the other wrist, stretched his arms out as far as they would go and pinned him to the sofa, relishing his gasp of surprise. Slowly she parted her legs, straddling him, letting the skirt of the velvet dress ride up a bit at a time as she inched along his thighs, teasing him, coming closer and closer until at last her moist, needy center connected with his hot hardness. He groaned.

"Gotcha," she whispered in his ear, then lightly darted her tongue into it, feeling him jolt beneath her, growing even hotter as he instinctively arched into her. "Isn't this more fun?" she'd meant to say, but it was hard to speak, hard to think, hard to do anything but focus on satisfying that one part of her body. She was giving way. She couldn't play her game much longer.

"Let me up, woman, and I'll show you fun." The words buzzed in her ears.

"Never." She paused for breath. "You are my prisoner and I intend to have my way with you."

She felt the strength in his arms, the energy in his muscles. He could release himself without the slightest effort, but instead, he bucked and fought beneath her, driving the flames higher and higher.

She licked little kisses across his face, pressed her aching breasts into his chest, the nipples tight against the velvet of her dress. It was going out of control, this game. It was missing—his hands, yes, the feel of his hands on her, and at last she let him go, feeling those hands go instinctively to her buttocks to tug her more tightly against him. They closed on bare skin, and a growl came from deep inside him.

"You temptress," he muttered, running his fingertips in circles over her, darting them beneath her, driving her to near insanity. "You little seductress, you shameless tart."

"Sticks and stones," she said, barely able to speak. Sitting back on his hands, she reached toward the end table, and in seconds, with the efficiency she had applied to every aspect of her life, all her life, she had smoothed a condom over him, feeling him throb beneath her fingers. Still holding him gently, she guided him into herself with one, swift, impatient, less than gentle thrust.

They moaned together as he drove deep inside her. With impatient fingertips he skimmed her dress up and over her head, crushing her naked breasts against his chest when he'd freed them. She buried her face in his shoulder and let the storm begin, the deep, thunderous roll, the flash of lightning, the funnel cloud picking her up and whirling her, whirling, whirling—

She screamed as spasms racked her body, at last whirling her beyond reality and into air so thin she could hardly hear the roar that came from him as he exploded inside her.

Exhausted, panting, they lay collapsed against the sofa cushions. He held her tight, rocking her against him, their sweat-slicked bodies sliding against each other, as the waves of sensation rippled through her one after the other, finally slowing, leaving her in a state of peaceful satiation.

Gently he eased both of them down until they were locked side by side the full length of the sofa. He breathed a long, deep sigh into her hair.

"Want to start on your fingernails?" he said at last, sounding as though he'd just gotten back his voice.

She felt the laughter of pure joy deep inside her. "No."

"Put that stuff on your hair that turns it brown?"

"No."

They lay in silence. Thinking about bed, she felt too tired to go to the trouble of getting there. Her eyes were closing all by themselves. All she could see were the twinkling lights from the Christmas tree making the tinsel glitter, the flickering candles.

"What was this all about, Sam?" she said sleepily, stretching out a little against him. "The tree and the eggnog and the Christmas carols?"

It took him so long to answer she was afraid she might have awakened him. "What was on my mind, I guess," he finally murmured, "was that if we couldn't have everything, at least we could have part of it."

"It was a good idea," Hope said, and tilted her head up for one last kiss.

9

SAM WENT HOME at dawn. His apartment seemed even more cheerless than usual as he showered and shaved, then opened the doors of his jumbled closet to select one of several expensively tailored suits that hung so incongruously there.

Keep up a good front. Spend what you had to on limousines, trendy restaurants, orchestra seats at Broadway plays, a single good watch, Italian shoes, carefully planned charitable donations. That case of wine from www.burgundy.com—he'd stick the bottles into silver foil bags and hand them out to Phil, to Cap, to ten more of his colleagues. *Blow it all out when it matters. Save in ways nobody will notice.* That was his mantra.

By renting this apartment instead of a classy condo, by claiming he was too busy for weekends in Paris, skiing in Gstaad or renting summer places in the Hamptons, by cooking for himself when he wasn't on an expense account, in the six years he'd been at Brinkley Meyers he'd finally paid off his college debts and established college funds for his four nephews. When he made partner, he'd be on top of the world.

Alone, there on top of the world.

His message light was blinking, and he pushed the play button to listen while he fastened cuff links into his shirt.

"Hi, baby." It was his mother. "Haven't heard from you in a while. We'll see you for Christmas, right? Give us a call and let Dad know when to pick you up at the airport."

Sam cursed softly. He still hadn't bought his ticket.

Hope was going home for Christmas. He knew she'd come from Chicago, had two sisters and her mother did Christmas up big. That was about it. There was so much he didn't know about her.

And would probably never learn. He had to get a lid on Hope, fasten it down with strapping tape and hide the Exacto knife until... Maybe forever, unless she...

Yeah, better use strapping tape. Next he realized he was wondering what she might like for Christmas. He gave his tie a vicious wrench.

An hour later he was at the office facing a stack of boxes labeled "Stockwell Plumbing Contractors vs. Palmer Pipe, Inc." Documentation on the case informally known as "Magnolia Heights."

"This is almost all of them," said the clerk who'd brought in one load after another on a dolly. He was a kid still in undergraduate school who undoubtedly aspired to be just like Sam Sharkey. Sam supposed now wasn't the time to warn him against it.

"Almost," Sam murmured.

"Just a couple more loads." He wheeled the dolly around and almost wiped out Cap Waldstrum, who was on his way into Sam's office.

"Congratulations," Cap said, neatly sidestepping. "I hear you got the big case."

"Seems like it. Either that, or I've been fired to make room to store the case documents."

"Not bloody likely." Cap's laugh sounded forced. "You're the crown prince around here these days."

"Because I got this case?"

"Because you're in the right place at the right time to take this case. I tried to reach you this weekend," Cap went on before Sam could say anything. "Didn't leave a message. Guess you were out and about."

"Yes," Sam said. "Out and about."

Cap hesitated. "Still seeing Hope Sumner?"

"As often as possible."

"Quite a coincidence she's at Palmer."

"Yes." Sam wished he knew where the conversation was heading. Most of all he wished Cap would get out of his office and let him start digging into the case.

"Who'd you say fixed the two of you up?"

Sam dropped all his plans to get to work and stared hard at Cap. "Mutual friends," he said, while trying to transmit the message, "and it's none of your damned business anyway."

Cap's eyes shifted away. "Small world, huh? Her being at Palmer and you getting the case."

Sam stood up. He wasn't all that much taller and sure wasn't any broader than Cap, but he noticed that Cap flinched. "Are you suggesting I'm seeing Hope in order to get this case?" He decided to put it all out on the table. "That I've been seeing Hope to get to Benton so he'd ask the firm to put me on the case?"

One thing he could say for Cap, he had finesse. "Hell, no, man," Cap said with an air of utter disbelief. "In fact, the reason I was trying to get in touch was to tell you I'd like to carry over from Corporate Division to the litigation team you're setting up. I was pretty involved in the settlement attempt. I'd like to see the thing through."

It caught him off guard, and Sam felt stunned. Cap was offering to follow Sam's orders? Be a member of

Sam's team instead of leading a team of his own? "Well, thanks, Cap," he said. "I'll know in a day or two what kind of support I need. It'd be good to have somebody who knows the facts from the inside out. I'll give you a call." He paused for what he hoped was just the right amount of time. "How's Muffy?" he said. "And the kids? All fired up for Christmas? You staying home, or going to Muffy's folks in Connecticut?"

Something in the way his mind was working right now—half on target, half back in bed with Hope—made him dial the airline as soon as Cap retreated. He made a reservation for Omaha on December twenty-third. For two. Just in case.

SHE WAS WEARING one of Hope Sumner's dress-for-success suits, in Hope Sumner's office, sitting at Hope Sumner's desk, so why couldn't she summon up Hope Sumner, Corporate Woman? All she could summon up were feelings from parts of her body that didn't have the faintest interest in pipe, that kept reminding her of the joys of the real thing.

Sam. Sam was the real thing.

But Sam was another stopgap measure. He wasn't part of the life she'd chosen, her real life. She'd promised herself she'd regain her focus or die trying.

The time had come. Focus or die.

Just the right time for the phone to ring. "Slidell!" Hope couldn't keep the surprise out of her voice. She hadn't supposed Slidell or any of his henchpersons knew how to use anything as arcane as a telephone.

"How's the loaner doing?"

"It's okay. Hasn't let me down yet." *Giving me more than I asked for.* Benton's e-mail was still arriving on her laptop. "When will I get my laptop back?"

"You missed the memorial service for your laptop," Slidell said. "I ordered you a new one. It'll be a few days. Want the optional two-hundred-twenty-five-dollar padded case?"

"Two hundred twenty-five?" Hope gasped. "The price went up? Did they add twenty-five dollars worth of padding?"

"No. So do you want it or not?"

"No. If it didn't work when it cost two hundred dollars it's not going to work at two twenty-five either. The computer I hired it to protect is, well, dead." *Rest in peace.*

It was time for Slidell to hang up, but he didn't. "Just wanted to be sure the loaner was taking up the slack," he said.

"As I said, it's doing just fine."

The silence hung between them. "So, thank you," Hope prompted him. He'd made the call. It was up to him to end it. But Slidell couldn't be expected to know the fine points of telephone etiquette.

When he finally broke the silence, he said, "Okey-dokey. It's yours for the duration. Make the most of it." With that surprising declaration, he hung up.

Make the most of it. Hope stared at the monitor screen. A tiny, high-pitched chord sounded from the computer and an e-mail message popped up on the screen. Hers? No, Benton's.

Make the most of it. Open Benton's messages.

She couldn't safely open the ones he hadn't read, but she could open the ones he *had* read and he'd never know. Her fingers froze on the keys. She couldn't invade Benton's privacy. It was considerably more than impolite, unprofessional and dishonest. It was illegal.

It was also the only way to find out if the frantic

exchange of messages meant there was something wrong with the plumbing pipe in Magnolia Heights. Still she hesitated.

A low buzz and a flashing light indicated an inter-office phone call. "Mr. Quayle would like to see you when you have a minute," Benton's secretary said.

"I'm flexible for the next half hour," Hope said. "Shall I come in now?" Get it over with, whatever it was?

First she closed the screen without reading Benton's message, then stepped briskly down the hall to his office, shoulders straight, head high. As for how she really felt, certain technical problems made it difficult for her to walk in carrying her own head on a silver platter, but if she could've, she would've.

"HOPE," BENTON SAID in his welcoming voice when she'd settled herself into a chair across from him.

She nodded, smiled a brief greeting, then dropped the smile. "I'm afraid the news is out. We're going to court in the Magnolia Heights case. I know this is a worry for you."

Closing in on the age of sixty, Benton was beginning to develop jowls, and when he nodded, he looked a lot like a bull terrier. "It is a worry, yes, indeed," he said.

"One thing we know we can count on," Hope said, "is Number 12867. It simply can't be the problem."

He managed a slight smile. "That's one of the reasons I asked to see you," he said. "I appreciate your loyalty to the company. I know I can count on you."

"Why, thank you, Benton," Hope said, guilty thoughts of his e-mail strumming hard against her temples. "You know how I feel about Palmer. It's like my family."

"Yes, yes." He contemplated her from under a furrowed brow. "And your loyalty will be rewarded, Hope, you can depend on that."

Her breath caught in her throat. Did he mean she'd be the next vice president for Marketing? "Palmer has always rewarded its people generously for their work," she said, and meant it. Her raises had come swiftly and consistently. She was making more money now than she knew what to do with.

"So I can continue to count on you, whatever happens?"

Something in his tone put her on the alert. "Why, yes, but what could possibly happen? We're in for a bad stretch here," she went on, "but we know the pipe's not at fault."

Benton looked grim. "Of course not, of course not," he said, "but I'm afraid we have someone here at Palmer without your kind of loyalty. Not naming any names, not making any definite accusations, but, well, some things have happened."

Somebody deleted one of your e-mail messages and you missed an important, hush-hush meeting? Hope could feel the tips of her ears turning red and was grateful that her hair covered them. "I'm sorry to hear that."

Benton's jowls quivered again, then he brightened a little. "Your nice young man will be arguing our case. You and he are still, ah, seeing each other?"

"Yes. I mean, it's not a serious thing yet, but we like each other's company. We're both so busy, you know."

He hardly seemed to hear what she was saying. "He's moving up at Brinkley Meyers same way you are at Palmer. This case could make his reputation. And with you there to remind him that what's good for Palmer's good for him..."

Her alarm increased. It occurred to her that Benton had used the word "loyalty" repeatedly in this strange conversation so full of euphemism, so fraught with hidden meanings. Loyalty implied more than hard work toward a common set of goals. Loyalty implied that you'd defend your liege whether he was right or wrong.

Was she prepared to defend Palmer right or wrong? Did she want the vice presidency that much?

What about Sam? Did he want the partnership that much?

She suddenly knew, without a doubt, that something was wrong in the Magnolia Heights case. But surely it had nothing to do with her. She wasn't a private investigator. She was merely a loyal employee. It wasn't up to her to find out what was wrong, or to act on it.

And Sam's job was to defend his client. Period.

"Benton," she said, hiding her fear and confusion, "my positive feelings in this case go deeper than my loyalty to Palmer. They have to do with my absolute faith in the quality of this pipe. If you're telling me there's something wrong with the pipe..."

Benton looked her straight in the eyes. "There's nothing wrong with the pipe."

"Good, then, because the worst thing you can do in a legal battle is not be completely up front with your lawyer. His job is to defend you, but he has to know what he's defending you against or he can't—"

Benton half-stood. "I know how lawyers work."

She'd already gone too far. She needed to mollify him and then leave as quickly as possible. "Of course you do." She smiled at him as she got to her feet, feeling dismissed. "I have absolute faith in the pipe—and in you."

"If you hear any rumors, anything I ought to know about, you will come straight to me about it, won't you?"

"Of course," Hope murmured.

If she thought he ought to know about it.

Her conviction that she'd just been offered the vice presidency increased when, later in the day, she saw St. Paul the Perfect emerge from Benton's office, grim-faced, a red flush high on his cheekbones. It didn't give her any satisfaction. It made her feel as though she'd somehow...

Cheated. By connecting herself to Sam? Ridiculous.

She went home early that evening, exhausted physically and emotionally, wanting Sam but not quite secure enough to call him and say, "Come over. Make it happen for me again, the warmth, the coziness, the passion. I want it all."

The sound she heard when she walked into her apartment made even her thoughts of Sam fade away, chilling her to the very marrow of her bones. The sound of water dripping.

"Leak!" she screamed. "Water leak!"

Thinking warped floors, streaked walls, melted wallpaper, wet rugs that would mildew before they dried, she darted into the kitchen, the powder room, the bathroom. She stepped out of the bathroom more slowly, puzzled by the absence of any sort of visible problem.

Drifting back into the living room, she moved toward the sofa. The sound increased. She thought of the game she and her sisters played on rainy days—"warmer, colder, warmer," until the blindfolded "It" eventually tagged her quarry. As she sat down on the sofa, the sound added a saucy gurgle to its music. Her head swiveled.

Maybelle had brought over something new. On a long narrow table she'd placed behind the sofa was a fountain, a large stone bowl into which water poured down a mini-waterfall beneath a tiny, perfect, bonsai tree.

Hope wiped her forehead, then sank it against the sofa cushions. A fountain. She'd thought broken pipes and it was just a fountain, another soothing influence for the frazzled working woman.

She'd thought broken pipes. She remembered the other things she'd thought about—the destruction of her possessions, the unpleasant moldy smell that would follow the soaking of the rugs and floors. The ugliness of the streaks and stains.

The residents of Magnolia Heights had been living in those conditions for months. No wonder they were angry. No wonder they wanted restitution.

That settled it. Tomorrow she would go to Magnolia Heights and see those conditions for herself.

But in the meantime...

She picked up the phone that sat on one of the new end tables and dialed Faith, reached her and then patched in to Charity. They pounced on her at once. "Who was there last night? Sam? That's great! Anything you'd like to tell us? Will you bring him home for Christmas?"—and on and on and on, blah, blah, blah, until Hope put the whole instrument on the new sofa table and turned on the speaker phone.

"What's that?" Charity said.

"I hear water running," Faith said.

"I'm in Niagara Falls," Hope said, then leaned back

against the sofa and smiled as she listened to their shrieks and cries of delight.

When they finally settled down, she said, "Just kidding. That's my new fountain."

Their cross exclamations made her smile even more vindictively. My, how she did love to push their buttons.

When the call ended, she examined the pipe star that still sat on the round table. It was quite dry now. She got the kitchen ladder, and stretching herself out to the limit, managed to position the star at the tip of the tree.

She stood back for a moment to admire it. To be perfectly honest, it looked more like a satellite than a star with its gold-sprayed center and the irregular lengths of pipe poking out of it, but it was stunning nonetheless, a tribute to creative thinking, and it hadn't cost more than five dollars in paint and Styrofoam.

There was a lot of love in it, though.

For a moment she let herself remember the time she and Sam had just spent together, feeling the sensations he aroused in her all over again, aching with want for him.

Could she have been thinking about him hard enough to make him call? Or was it possible he'd already been thinking about her? Whatever the reason, when the phone rang she knew it would be Sam.

"Hi," he said.

No more, "Hope? Sam." They knew each other's voices now. Intimately. But one thing hadn't changed. Now all it took was the word, "Hi," to make her blood run hot in her veins, to make her wriggle against the sofa cushions.

"Hi, Sam."

"Good day at the office?"

"It was okay. How about yours?"

The things unsaid vibrated in the air. His voice was low and husky. Hers, she knew, was different from the voice of Hope the professional woman.

"Okay here, too." He paused. "I got into the Magnolia Heights case today."

"How does it look?"

"Well..."

He seemed to be settling in somewhere, into something. She wondered where he was. Was he still at his office in his shirtsleeves with his tie loosely knotted, or was he at home, slouching around in a sweater and wool socks? She could hear a voice in the background, then simply a cacophony of noise. A television set? Or had he gone to a bar? With friends? After a flash of admittedly unjustified jealousy, she gave up trying to guess and waited to hear what he had to say.

"It's not going to be easy," he told her. "Lots of emotion tied up in this case, lots of sentiment, human interest. The media's having a good time with it. It's going to be hard to get a fair trial."

"But what's happened, however inconvenient for Magnolia Heights, wasn't the fault of Palmer Pipe. That's all you have to show, isn't it? That it wasn't the pipe?"

"You're thinking like a lawyer." He sounded amused.

"No," she said, "I'm thinking like a potential vice president of Marketing." She gave him a brief rundown of her conversation with Benton, telling him only the good parts, leaving out the worrisome ones. "I'm thinking selfishly here."

"Me, too," he said, and sighed. Then, "Are you doing your girl stuff tonight? The masque and the hair gunk?"

Was she? "Nope," she said, surprising herself. "My face is fine, I can just keep patching up my fingernails and with five inches of snow on the ground, my toenails aren't much of an issue. I'm taking the night off."

"Good for you."

"And furthermore," Hope said, getting up to pace the room, "I'm not eating another one of those ghastly TV dinners. I'm going to order—" she paused to let her taste buds kick in "—Indian food!"

"For one or two?"

She halted in her pacing. She glanced at the star on top of the tree. She could already feel Sam's arms around her, taste the warm maleness of his skin, feel her fingers in his hair, on his shoulders, clutching him for dear life....

"Indian food's always more interesting for two," she said. "You can order a bunch of things to share. I, ah, don't suppose you'd like to..."

"Is that any way to make a sale?" Sam said. He mimicked her. "'I don't suppose you'd like to'?"

"Damn," Hope said. "I'll start over."

"Don't bother," Sam said. "I'm an easy mark. See you in—"

Silently he thrust a bill at the driver and got out of the cab. Smiling, remembering, he glanced through the doorway of Hope's apartment building and shifted the box of Christmas cookies to his other hand. "Two minutes."

He'd rather been looking forward to seeing her in the green masque again. It would seem like an anniversary.

10

IT WAS TOO LOVELY for words, waking up beside Sam. Waking up early this time, in the dark of a winter's morning. She'd mention curtains to Maybelle tonight, though, in case...in case Sam was still in her bed when spring came? Was it too much to hope for?

"Time is it?" He yawned sleepily.

"Five."

"Rise and shine."

"Rise, anyway."

He rolled over and took her in his arms, pulling her to him, molding her naked body against his. He stroked her back, buried his face in her neck. "I have risen," he said solemnly, proving it as he tugged her even more tightly against him. "It's time to get up, and I've gotten up. But now I have to go home." With obvious regret, he rolled away.

"Have some coffee before you go," Hope said.

"Love some. Mind if I shower here? Saves a step."

"Make yourself at home." She smiled at him.

He joined her ten minutes later, wearing yesterday's clothes, while she'd bundled herself into her warm, sexless white robe and slippers. She poured the coffee and put out the cinnamon rolls she hadn't served him on Sunday morning.

"As long as we're here," he said, sounding less

sleepy, "let's coordinate our schedules." He pulled out his Palm Pilot.

"Um," Hope mumbled through the first bite of cinnamon roll, then retrieved her Palm Pilot from its cradle. She wished she had a camera to capture for posterity the two of them sitting at the small round table in the living room, each scribbling on the screen of his own personal Palm Pilot. It was such a cozy scene.

"No parties tonight, right?"

"No. And I've asked Maybelle to meet me here at seven."

"The decorator?"

"Yes. Maybelle Ewing."

It amused her when he automatically punched the address list icon with his stylus and wrote down the name. "Tell her I like whatever it is she's done to this place."

"I'll do that."

"Especially the fountain. I bet you like it, too. It's got pipe in it." He gave her one of his villainous smiles.

"Enough already," she snapped with an irritation she didn't feel, and he knew it.

"Okay," he said, "about tomorrow night..."

"The party one of our customers is giving." She cocked her head to one side. "Please don't tell me you can't go. I've really been counting on you," she said, and added all in a rush, "The CEO's wastrel son works for his father in a position where he can't do much harm." She paused briefly. "He liaisons with me. Anyway, the CEO has all but asked me if I earn enough to support two in the manner to which his son has become accustomed."

Sam's eyes flashed a little. "It's on my schedule. *Nothing* will keep me from going."

"Thank goodness."

"Thursday. Oh, yeah, that's the party at Cap's house out in New Jersey."

Hope's ears perked up. "I'm looking forward to that one. I get to meet Mrs. Cap."

"And I get to sidestep Mrs. Cap's...I mean Muffy's...sister, who will almost certainly be there to look you over."

Hope quirked an eyebrow. "Is a new outfit called for?"

"Do you have anything from Fredericks of Hollywood?"

"No, and it's too late to order. I'll have to discourage her hopes and dreams with the sheer force of my personality." She hesitated. "Unless you might be interested some time in the future."

"I don't think so," Sam replied.

"Friday night. Friday night," she said, answering her own question, "you get to meet the people I call my friends."

In answer to the curious look he gave her, she said, "We see each other maybe twice a year because nobody has time for more than that. We call it being friends."

"All you can have for now," Sam murmured.

"You have some of those, too?"

"Oh, yes. You'll meet most of them at Cap's party. I don't get out of my own tank much."

"Okay, then, we're set for now."

"And a week from today is Christmas."

"That soon?" Hope said, feeling panicked.

"When are you going home?"

"Saturday. You?"

"Sunday."

They gazed at each other.

"I don't suppose..." They spoke together.

"...you'd like to go home with me, instead," Sam finished for both of them. His smile was wry.

"Home *is* where I feel the worst pressure," Hope said. "Taking you with me would keep my mom and sisters quiet on the all-work-and-no-play battlefront."

"Exactly what went through my mind," Sam said.

"But we can't be two places at once," Hope said.

"Nope." Sam got up and took his cup and plate to the kitchen, where he put them directly into the dishwasher. "I don't want to, but I've got to get going."

"Big day?" Hope said, joining him with her dishes.

"Long day. For you, too, I bet." He took the dishes out of her hands and added them to his. "Bye," he said, tipping her chin up and giving her a light, brushing kiss before springing into action in the way that was quintessentially Sam, coat, scarf, gloves, briefcase—gone.

For just a moment, Hope sank down into one of the armchairs, letting the full set of conflicting feelings consume her. Then she marched into her office alcove, resolutely connected her laptop to her second phone line, logged into the network—and watched a message to Benton pop up on the screen in the corner.

The message was from Cap Waldstrum.

Hope stared at it. *Loyalty. Professional behavior. Truth.* She opened it.

"Confirming. Same time, same place. Don't be late."

This time she didn't delete it. If Benton opened it at home, it might appear as a new, unread message. If he downloaded it from the office network, he would see it had been read. Whatever happened would happen.

"YOU'RE GOING OUT to lunch?"

"Yes," Hope said, breezing past the administrative assistant's desk.

"Business, of course."

"Of course," Hope said, feeling paranoid enough to eye the woman suspiciously for a second. But all she saw was a teasing smile, not unlike the smile Charity would be giving her under the same circumstances.

All work, no play. Now that she was playing a little bit, she'd discovered they were right. The part of her life where Sam lived felt great.

For now.

Get on with it. This is not the time to think about Sam.

From the building in midtown that housed Palmer Pipe, Hope darted into Saks, made a beeline for the Ladies Lounge and dived into her overstuffed briefcase. She emerged looking less like a Saks customer than she had when she walked in. Unless the observer happened to know how expensive her sneakers were, or that the scarf over her hair was from Hermes.

Huddled inside her oldest coat, she practically jogged the long block to Sixth Avenue and the D Train. At Columbus Circle she changed to the A train, and soon emerged several blocks from Magnolia Heights, three huge buildings rising out of a snowy plot of land from which a few young, sad-looking trees and shrubs poked up their heads.

She selected the middle building. Talk about dumb, she scolded herself, she'd expected to find a doorman waiting. Faced instead with a block of names, each with a buzzer beside it, she took a deep breath and pushed the first buzzer her finger landed on.

There was no answer. She chose another buzzer. No answer. On the fifth try, a woman's voice answered. A baby cried in the background. Hope almost gave up her plan then and there, but not quite.

"Hello?" she said. "Sorry to bother you, but I'm Sally Sue Sumner? A social worker?" Hearing the uncertainty in her voice, she winced. If she'd descended to disguise and deception to get at the truth, she had to do a better job of it. "I'm on a committee to determine the health hazards of the water damage here. May I have a minute of your time?"

There was a long silence, except for the baby crying. "Well, I guess so," said the woman. "Come on up."

A wonderful sound came from the locked front doors—a long, loud buzz and a click, and she'd done it. She was inside the building and on her way up in a Spartan, but new and clean, elevator to Apartment 7H, where, according to the name plate, a family named Hotchkiss lived.

Mrs. Hotchkiss was young and rather pretty. She bounced an adorable baby on her shoulder, a little girl, Hope thought, who seemed to be abandoning her earlier tears and going for sleep, instead. "Teething," said the woman, nodding at the baby.

Hope gave her a look of pure womanly understanding. She knew nothing about teething, but understood it was horrible for the parents. Perhaps horrible for the child as well, but so far she'd only heard the parents' side of the story.

"Thanks for seeing me," Hope said.

"I should ask you for an identification card or something," Mrs. Hotchkiss said, looking nervous.

"Of course," Hope said reassuringly, and reached confidently into her handbag. *Think of something, think of something.* With her hand still groping at the bottom of the bag, she looked up toward the ceiling. "Omigosh," she said.

Her reaction was genuine, although she'd only looked skyward to pray for a miracle. She'd gotten her miracle. Mrs. Hotchkiss forgot all about her need for Hope's identification. "Pretty, isn't it?" she said.

Hope was sure she'd meant to sound sarcastic instead of sad. The ceiling they both gazed at bore a large, dark spot. Over the spot, paint made bubbles, then cracked. The ceiling itself seemed to sag a little, which explained the rather odd placement of the furniture. Although the room was small, everything in it was crammed into the side away from the ominous-looking spot. The floor was bare.

"It's better now that it stopped dripping," said Mrs. Hotchkiss.

"I'm sure it is," Hope said weakly. "So, Mrs. Hotchkiss, how long has this situation been going on?"

Having already wormed her way in, Hope let the woman talk as long as she wanted to. When her tale of woe finally ran down, Hope said, "Do you know any of your neighbors?"

"Some of them," Mrs. Hotchkiss said. "Mainly the ones with little kids. We walk our babies together, and baby-sit for each other."

"Would you be willing to introduce me to a few of them?"

"Sure," said Mrs. Hotchkiss, and reached for her phone.

Hope left the building shaken. She'd seen everything she'd imagined the night before when she'd walked into her apartment to hear the tinkling of her own lovely little fountain—the mold, the mildew, the warped floors, the buckled asphalt tiles, the soaked rugs these people couldn't afford to throw away.

Mushrooms were growing in the corner of one of the apartments. When the women asked Hope what she thought they should do about their living conditions, the answer that popped out of her mouth was, "Don't eat the mushrooms."

She'd left promising to do something to help them. What an empty promise. What could she possibly do?

Because it simply wasn't the pipe. On that one point she could not, would not, back down.

She went out through the front door, wrapping her old coat tightly around her when the cold wind hit, and came to an abrupt standstill, staring at the big plate of names and buzzers. The name that caught her eye was Hchiridski.

There couldn't be that many Hchiridskis in the world, not in this part of the world, anyway. Slidell's family? Slidell's mom? Did people like Slidell have moms?

If the Hchiridskis who lived at Magnolia Heights were in fact Slidell's family, a lot of things came clear. Shaking her head, feeling a headache start up at her temples, she looked out toward the street and froze. Getting out of a taxi at the curb was Sam, and with him, Cap Waldstrum.

Hope spun, huddled under her Hermes scarf, slumped her shoulders and hurried off toward the building to the north.

While Cap paid the cab fare, collecting, of course, the receipt to submit for reimbursement, Sam watched the figure scuttling away in the opposite direction.

It was amazing what a little work could do for a

woman. Now that woman—if she'd do something about her posture, she'd remind him a lot of Hope.

He was afraid the time was quickly coming when he'd have to live with mere memories of Hope. Because the more he got into the data, the surer he was that the problem at Magnolia Heights was directly related to Palmer Pipe, and attacking Palmer Pipe was one and the same as attacking Hope.

He might also be living with mere memories of having once been *that close* to a partnership at Brinkley Meyers. No way would he get it if he upset the carefully constructed case against Stockwell Plumbing Contractors by discovering that his client had been lying.

He was meeting an engineer at Magnolia Heights today because he had to know the truth, even if he made a decision not to act on it.

He cast a glance at Cap. Cap, who was carefully tucking the receipt into a special pocket of his briefcase, couldn't possibly know what was going through his mind. Sam had accepted Cap's offer and put him on the litigation team. It was the best way to keep an eye on him.

Because something was wrong about Cap, too, and Sam wanted to be there, swimming just beneath the surface, when Cap dangled his legs once too often.

They didn't call him The Shark for nothing.

But Sam wasn't an eating machine. He hated what he was doing. What hurt worst was that he couldn't talk any of this over with Hope. And, God help him, how he wanted to.

"BENTON, I'M SO GLAD I caught you," Hope said at five-thirty that evening. "Do you have a minute?" With the receiver to her ear, she directed her gaze toward the sheet of paper on her desk.

"Not much more than a minute," Benton said. He didn't sound enthusiastic, which made her think she was on the right track.

"I'll be right there," Hope promised him, tossing the paper—her plan of action—into her bottom drawer and snatching up the ad for Number 12867 she planned to run in an engineering journal the following summer.

It was her excuse for visiting Benton. Her real reason was to see if he seemed to be heading for a mysterious meeting in a mysterious place. To see if he'd noticed that someone had read an e-mail message of his. To make whatever was going to happen happen as quickly as possible. She was ready to get it over with and get on with her life. Which, she feared, would never be the same again.

"So what do you think of this?" Hope said a few minutes later. "Too aggressive with just that one word, 'Invincible' monopolizing the page?"

Benton had a worried look about him, seemed to be having difficulty concentrating. "No, no I don't think...I mean, I think it's fine, makes its point..."

"It's for *American Engineer*," Hope said. "I didn't think we wanted to distract engineers with too many words. Just the one sound byte, 'Palmer Pipe is invincible.' Of course, on the other hand..."

She was rattling on, hoping for signs of impatience on his part. And eventually they appeared.

"Discuss the options with the ad agency tomorrow," he finally muttered. "Sorry. Hate to rush you, but I have a six o'clock meeting."

She leaped up. "I'm sorry. I've been so thoughtless.

It's just that you have such insight into these things I always like to run my ideas past you. I'll talk to the agency right away. So," she said, giving him a bright smile at the doorway, "have a nice evening."

She flew down the hallway and shouldered her briefcase, which she'd repacked when she changed again at Saks, where she felt they were getting to know her. She had no time for a transformation now. With any luck she could get into the scarf and change coats.

Because she was going to follow Benton to his assignation. She had exactly enough time to do that and still get home to meet Maybelle.

Once you started misbehaving, it was hard to quit.

She emerged from the building a mere ten steps behind Benton, who seemed so intent on his own thoughts he was unlikely to notice her. Her excitement grew when he set out walking instead of getting into the chauffeured car that was one of his perks at Palmer. While she trailed him, she put on her scarf. At a red light, she ducked into a shoe store doorway, got the old coat out of the briefcase and managed to get it on before the light changed.

The briefcase still dangled open as she pursued him two more blocks south, gradually getting her other coat stuffed in and the zipper zipped.

How did real spies do it, she wondered? Surely not this clumsily. She'd pick herself out as a person bent on mischief in a millisecond.

Benton paused in front of the Donnell Library on Fifty-third Street, and to her amazement, went in. With some temerity, she followed. While she squinted at the large-print books, trying to look as if she needed one, he went up the stairs to the mezzanine. She waited a short interval, then followed.

She found him at a table in the reference section. Alone. It was still five minutes before six. A minute or so later, a man she recognized, an executive with Stockwell Plumbing Contractors, sat down at a nearby table without acknowledging Benton's presence.

Hope, who'd developed a sudden interest in Art and Architecture, hovered between the stacks, her heart pounding in her chest. She'd gotten through Georgian architecture and Gothic Revival, and had worked her way down to Frank Lloyd Wright when, at last, the scene reached the punchline.

Cap Waldstrum came through the elevator doors and glanced around the room.

Hope hunched her shoulders around a book entirely devoted to the Johnson and Johnson building, one of Mr. Wright's most famous structures. When she dared to look up again, Cap had selected a book and had seated himself opposite the executive from Stockwell.

Fortunately, Frank Lloyd Wright had built a lot of famous buildings, some of them described in books that were lighter in weight than the Johnson and Johnson book. She selected one of them, and when she peered out over the top of it, Cap was sliding the book toward himself, taking something out from under it and putting that something—an envelope—into his briefcase.

She held her breath. She knew what would happen next and she couldn't bear it. He replaced the book on the shelf, picked up another one and sat down opposite Benton.

An unaccustomed emotion assailed Hope. It was fear. When was the last time she'd felt afraid?

When she'd stood in the hallway of their real parents' house on the day of the funeral, clutching her sisters' hands, listening to her grandmother and aunts planning to split them up. Knowing their mother wanted them to run—run to the arms of her childhood friend, Maggie Sumner, who would love them all, would keep them together. Knowing it was up to her to get them there.

She tugged herself back into the present just in time to see Benton hand yet another envelope to Cap. Sick at heart, Hope sneaked out from the stacks, took the stairs and sped toward the subway.

MAYBELLE WAS right on time and absolutely out of control about the Christmas tree. "I couldn't hardly believe it when I snuck in with that fountain and found a tree sittin' there all decorated up so purty! And you did it without me even saying, 'Get a Christmas tree, hon, it'll make you happy.'"

"I didn't do it all by myself," Hope said. "Have some coffee." She was surprised to notice she'd also poured herself a cup of the real stuff, and furthermore, that she intended to drink it down to the last drop. Maybe have a second cup, she thought recklessly. She wouldn't sleep a wink. But she wouldn't have anyway. She was too worried.

"My, this is good coffee," Maybelle enthused further. "What's wrong, hon?"

The question came so abruptly that Hope felt like a basketball player who'd just felt the ball land in his hands and had no choice but to shoot.

"Why didn't you and Hadley get along?" she asked. It wasn't what she'd intended to say. She'd intended to ask Maybelle deep questions about ethics and morals, about when to speak up and when to stay silent, and she'd chosen her sounding board wisely, because it was clear that Maybelle tended to speak up.

Instead, all she could think about was Sam and what the probability was that they could ever have a long-lasting—like forever—relationship, because if they couldn't, it didn't much matter what she did about the Magnolia Heights case. If they could, she had an even worse short-term problem.

Because what the scene at the library had looked like was Cap blackmailing Benton and the man from Stockwell, and there could only be one reason. There was something wrong with Number 12867. Benton and the Stockwell company knew something was wrong. Cap had found out something was wrong—and they were paying him to keep quiet. And if Sam defended Palmer without knowing the facts, it could ruin him, not make his reputation.

"I feel like I kinda lost you somewhere," Maybelle said.

"I'm sorry," she said. "We were talking about you and Hadley."

"No, you were." But Maybelle smiled, briefly at least. And then she sighed. "Oh, sugar, me and Hadley came from another generation. When we met I was a rodeo rider—"

"Really?" Hope breathed, distracted at last. "You mean bucking broncos and mad bulls and..."

"No. I was one of the pretty girls in the pretty outfits ridin' pretty horses who decorated the place while the men rode the bucking broncos and the mad bulls."

"I hear you," Hope said.

"So we fell in love—or lust, you young folks call it—and got married. And all of a sudden he didn't want to be married to a rodeo rider."

"He wanted to be married to..." Hope prompted her.

"A lady his Mamma would approve of," Maybelle said, looking a bit regretful for once. "A housewife. A mother. A good Christian canner."

"A what?"

"A person who cans her own food."

"Oh, my gosh," Hope said. She didn't even cook her own food. She didn't heat soup or bake the TV dinners. What she couldn't manage with Zabars so close, a microwave oven at hand, and the phone number of Food in Motion, an excellent catering service, simply wouldn't happen. Ever.

"I didn't do so hot at the housewife or the canning part," Maybelle said. Her voice softened. "I would've liked to be a mother. But I guess I just couldn't, and that was before all this fertility stuff came around."

"I'm sorry," Hope said. The same people who'd told her about the horrors of teething had told her about their earlier fertility problems.

"So things went wrong right up front and we just never got it together," Maybelle finished up.

"And then Hadley tackled a bull and died?"

"Not exactly, hon," Maybelle said. "The bull went for me, and Hadley threw himself between us. He never knew what hit him." She thought for a moment. "Well, he must know now it was the bull."

"He loved you no matter what," Hope said faintly.

"With just a little talkin', a little honesty, we might've been okay," Maybelle said. "The feng shui, that might have made the talkin' easier. So what's with your young man?"

Again, her question caught Hope off guard and sent her rattling on without thinking. "I have to decide what honesty will do to him. Then I have to decide what *I* would do to him, his goals, that is. And unfortunately—" she turned a pleading face toward Maybelle "—what his goals would do to me."

"You said that real nice," Maybelle complimented her. Then, to Hope's dismay, she stood up. "Thanks again, hon, for the coffee and the talk. And your Christmas tree's just gorgeous! What's that star made out of? Pipe? Whoo-ee, that's pure Martha Stewart."

"Maybelle."

The woman halted, turned.

"Who should I be loyal to? To Palmer? To Sam? To those people at Magnolia Heights?"

Maybelle looked puzzled. "Why, to yourself, hon. That's a no-brainer." She left, wearing a mammoth coat that looked suspiciously like coyote.

Loyal to herself. What the heck did that mean?

Now Hope was certain she wouldn't sleep tonight.

11

"WHAT ARE YOU SO nervous about?" Sam said.

"Nothing!"

Something. Her voice was high-pitched, and she'd almost jumped out of her skin when he spoke. The entire trip to Upper Montclair, New Jersey, she'd been wound up like that.

"Don't worry about Cap," he reassured her. "He won't come on to you. He appreciates pretty women, but he's got too much invested in his life with Muffy."

"That's a funny way to put it. Invested."

"You'll know what I mean when you see the house. Muffy's designer dress. The two kids in their little five hundred dollar party outfits just for saying hello in before the nanny takes them off to bed. If you can think of a reason to sneak out to the garage—" He slid his hand up her silky leg from the ankle to the sensitive spot he'd found just above her kneecap, indicating that he could think of a reason to sneak out to the garage. "You'll find a BMW and a Porsche, and a Jeep for slumming around in." She'd shivered at his touch, but the shiver felt more like a shudder.

"It sounds like an expensive life," she said. "How can he afford it?" She'd lowered her voice enough that it didn't actually pierce the old eardrum, but it was still tight.

"The firm pays us well," he told her. It was something he'd often wondered himself. "Muffy's family's well-to-do and so is Cap's. I doubt that he saves much, but I don't think he's paying off college loans, either."

He could see by the shadow of curiosity that crossed her face that she'd like to know if he had loans to pay off, but her manners were too good to let her ask. At this point, there was no reason she shouldn't know. "It felt great the day I paid off the last of mine," he said.

"You put yourself through school? That takes a lot of courage."

"Desperation," Sam said, pulling her close to him. "When my dad lost the farm he had to support us by working as a mechanic. Mom's a good manager, but things were always tight."

"That's hard," Hope said. "I can see why you want to succeed so badly."

"What about you? What's driving you?"

"I don't really know." It sounded like a confession. "Some of us just have that sort of personality, I guess. But my sisters and I went through a scary time together before Mom and Dad adopted us, and it was up to me to take care of us. Charity was too young to take charge, and Faith was too unorganized. I had to be the leader." Her smile was fond. "I've always thought that had some kind of effect on me, made me think the whole world depended on me."

He hugged her a little tighter. He wanted to ask about that "scary time," but the driver had pulled into a brightly lit circular driveway behind a line of limousines and they had arrived.

HOPE DREADED seeing Cap Waldstrum more than she'd ever dreaded seeing anybody. She suspected he'd see the accusation in her eyes without her having to say a word. Of course she wouldn't say a word. Not here. Not now.

Maybe not ever. She could keep her guilty secret and go on with her life. She was only guessing anyway. For all she knew, those envelopes Cap was packing away last night held—what could they have held besides money? You didn't call secret meetings at a library to sell raffle tickets in support of your favorite charity. Secret documents? Those three men were the good guys about to blow the whistle on the bad guys? *Dream on. It was money. Cap's blackmailing Palmer and Stockwell.*

The sleepless night she'd predicted and a depressingly unproductive day hadn't yielded any answers. She still didn't know what to do.

Sam had put Cap on his litigation team. What if Sam was keeping a guilty secret, too, just to get the partnership?

He certainly wasn't acting like a man with a guilty secret. "Muffy, gorgeous as always," he said, giving Muffy a real kiss on her cheek. "Hey, you guys." He knelt down to shake the children's hands. "What's Santa Claus bringing you this year?"

"Cap," he said next, clapping a hand on Cap's shoulder. "You remember Hope."

"I told you I couldn't possibly—"

Cap hesitated for a second, gazing at her, and Hope's heart rose to her throat and stuck there. Surely he hadn't seen her last night in the library.

"—forget her," he finished, still gazing.

Hope had played a minor role in the Senior Class play in high school. She now recalled that she'd been the worst actor in the play, maybe the worst actor in the history of the high school. The drama coach had said as much and had told Hope firmly that her future did not lie on the stage. Well, she would have to improve on that performance.

"Hello again, Cap," she said brightly. "Muffy, I'm so glad to meet you. And your children—" she mouthed the words as though the children might become unbearably vain on the basis of one compliment "—are adorable."

Muffy was small, blond and cute, and she didn't so much speak as bubble. Hope liked her instantly, which made her feel even worse about suspecting Cap of being a blackmailer. Muffy was, though, wearing the designer dress Sam had predicted she would, a confection of red chiffon and crystal beads, and her diamonds rivaled Ruthie Quayle's.

"Ooh, I've been wanting to meet you ever since Cap told me about you," Muffy said, sparkling all over. "First I was really disappointed, because I had my eye on Sam for my sister Cheryl." She gestured toward a woman who stood at the edge of the crowd, a woman who, though pretty enough and dressed in a sexy, trendy outfit, didn't sparkle like Muffy. "But now that I've met you—" She delivered herself of a deep sigh, which she followed up with a big smile of forgiveness. "I'll give up on that idea."

"Your sister's a very attractive—" Hope began, but Muffy bubbled right on.

"Isn't it the most amazing thing that you're at Palmer and Sam's at Brinkley Meyers and Cap's been working on the settlement?" Her pretty scarlet mouth formed into a pout. "He worked so hard on it, too. We didn't see him for weeks. And they still couldn't pull it off."

"Don't worry," Sam said blithely, "we'll win the case in court. Hope, I want you to meet..."

He steered her into the crowd. It was a large party, catered by a well-known Manhattan caterer. The Waldstrum Christmas tree stood twelve feet high in the marble-floored foyer of the impressive suburban house, and it showed a professional decorator's touch.

Nostalgia, a longing to return to her innocent childhood, flooded over Hope as she looked at it. The ornaments went all the way to the top, far higher than either of the Waldstrum children could reach.

Everywhere she looked she saw the stamp of money. Money well-spent—everything was in good taste. But it was also true that everything, including this party, had cost a fortune. In his early thirties, Cap was already living the high life.

She realized that she had no idea how Sam lived. She was sure, though, that he didn't live like this. Neither did she. But Cap supported a wife and two children in style on an undoubtedly similar salary. Family money? Trust funds? Or was he leveraged to the hilt? Even in financial trouble?

She thought and worried as she nodded and smiled at the approving gazes of Sam's friends. Just as any good piece of arm candy would do.

"THAT WAS A lovely party," she told Sam when they got back into the hired limousine.

"Muffy goes all out," Sam said. He slid closer to her, put his arm around her, stroked her shoulder through her coat.

She couldn't help leaning into his embrace, couldn't help sliding her hand across his chest. She could feel his heart beating, hear his breathing quicken. His mouth brushed her forehead. She closed her eyes.

A couple going home after a party. When they got

there, she'd set up the coffee for the next morning while he checked on the children, sweetly asleep because the nanny had put them to bed hours ago.

Then they'd get into bed with their laptops and Palm Pilots, and several hours later when they'd tied up the loose ends of their day, if they weren't too tired, they'd make love and it would be so wonderful.

The nanny would get the children up in the morning, too, and get them dressed and fed, because Mommy and Daddy, who'd gone straight to the party from work, would already have left for work again—

When did our children see us last?

Hope bolted upright in the back seat of the limousine.

"What?" Sam said.

Embarrassed, Hope mumbled, "Nothing," and snuggled back in. "Just something I forgot to do at the office."

"Must've been important." His mouth grazed her cheekbone, slid down her face.

What she'd forgotten were the names of the children they didn't have. Wonder how that news would grab him.

His mouth found hers in the darkness, took it lightly, briefly because they weren't alone, but it sent the heat flowing through her. The shock of his tongue darting into her mouth traveled down to her core with lightning speed. Her hand tightened on his jacket.

He drew back. She could feel the heat of his face, imagine the flush rising on it, knew he was aroused and wanting her as much as she wanted him.

He settled back with his arm slung across the top of the seat. Hope swallowed hard when she felt his other hand on her knee, whispered his name in a breathless warning as it sneaked up the inside of her thigh and then gasped aloud when his fingertips found their mark.

She opened her eyes wide. He returned her astonished gaze with the most innocent of smiles. "What are you *do*-ing?" she hissed at him.

"It's a long drive," he whispered back, sending the words directly into the shell of her ear and increasing the sensations that were taking on a life of their own. "I'm trying to entertain you."

"Couldn't you just sing?" With a little gasp she buried her face in his shoulder. "What will the driver think?"

"Nothing, if you'll stop leaping around like that." The amusement in his voice hummed through her hair as his fingers explored her through her sheer panty hose, through her black silk panties, stroking, teasing, making her feverish with wanting him to touch her directly, to share the heat, feel the moisture.

She sank her teeth into the fabric of his overcoat to muffle the moan rising in her throat.

His hand suddenly went to her waist and gripped the elastic of her panty hose. "If you'll lean back and lift up a little, dear, I'll straighten your coat out underneath you," he said in a loud, clear voice.

"Why, thank you, darling," Hope said, sounding strangled, which was exactly the way she felt. "You noticed I wasn't comfortable. Aren't you swe-e-e-e…"

The panty hose and panties locked her knees together now, but there was still room for Sam's large, strong hand, his smooth fingertips, and when he slipped his index finger inside her she writhed with pleasure.

"Still not comfortable, sweetheart?"

"Not. Quite." She was dying here, letting go, not caring what happened as long as his fingers kept on stroking and plunging, his thumb kept up its light touch on a nub so swollen and sensitive it seemed to have taken over her whole person.

"Here, let's try this," he murmured, and slid his hands under her bare buttocks as the spasms began to quake uncontrollably through her body and she buried her face again in his shoulder.

He waited a few minutes, still stroking, as wave after wave of euphoria crashed over her. "There," he said when she stilled. "Better now?"

"Much."

"Good."

"My panty hose are cutting off the circulation below my knees," she muttered a few minutes later, wondering why his inelegant snort of laughter was more exciting than another man's poetry.

She'd almost composed herself when at last they pulled up to her apartment building. "Want to come in for some coffee?" she asked him, sending messages with her eyes that had nothing to do with coffee. "And take a taxi home?" she added for the driver's benefit.

"Great idea," Sam said, hauling himself out after her.

He behaved himself all the way to her apartment, where he backed her up against the door and took her in his arms, hard, demanding.

"The key," she gasped, "the key..."

And then they were inside. The fountain plinked, the wind chimes tinkled, the Christmas tree glowed, and so did the message light on the answering machine. Hope was oblivious to everything but Sam, his hands on her skin, his mouth on her breasts, skimming her out of her dress, leaving it in a heap on the floor and making a trail of silk and lace, bow tie and boxer shorts, a trail that led into the bedroom.

They nestled together on the ivy-patterned sheets, giving, taking, caring for each other and accepting gifts for themselves until their bodies forged into one and began the long, sweet spin, going out of control, flying off into space together and at last, slowly, settling down to the warm, moist arms of a welcoming Earth.

HOPE WOKE UP, reached out an arm to snuggle it around Sam and found he was no longer beside her. She heard noises, though, clanking sounds, and got up to investigate.

She crept across the living-room floor toward the light that shone out of the storage closet. She noticed in passing that Sam had folded their clothes, and also that most of his still seemed to be there, so he hadn't gone far. In fact, he was the most likely person to be in her closet. Why he was in the closet was the question.

She peered in through the door and found him sitting cross-legged on the floor in his tucked shirt and boxer shorts playing with pipe.

"Just couldn't wait for Santa Claus, could you," she said, resting on her knees beside him.

"Is this Number 12867?" he asked, holding up a short, stocky white length of PVC.

"That's my baby."

He held up a ninety-degree angle joint. "Is this what you use to join the pieces together?"

"Yes, straight pieces or various angles. Notice that the joint is a lot thicker than the pipe, twice as thick, actually..." She halted. "Is the middle of the night really the best time to learn about pipe?"

At last he directed a sexy smile at her. "I thought any time was good for you."

"Hush. Why the curiosity?"

He was serious again. "Because somebody's got to figure out what went wrong. Here we have this state-of-the-art pipe, and it's leaking."

"It isn't. Well, I mean it is, but it just can't be." The time she'd spent at Magnolia Heights, the things she'd seen, came back to her in a rush. "The plumbing contractor just didn't screw it in right," she insisted.

"How do you make pipe?"

"Oh, for heaven's sake!"

"I know, sort of, from reading the briefing documents. I just thought you might say something I hadn't heard before."

She futzed around getting her bare feet tucked under her cuddly white robe, grumbling all the while, then said, "They buy these polyvinyl chloride pellets. Then they put the pellets in a vat and melt them down and stir the whole mess up, then they pour it into dies—molds, like Jell-O molds or—"

"I know what dies are."

"—dies they've installed in the machines and when it cools down you've got pipe."

"No need to overdramatize it," Sam said.

"Well, that's all there is to it." She was still grumbling.

"Then what's so special about Number 1286?"

"Some secret components of the pellets. Special dies. This and that."

"So there are a couple of things that could go wrong. The wrong pellets, the wrong temperature, maybe, they used to melt them down, the stirring up process, whatever that is, or a flaw in the dies. Have I got that straight?"

"You haven't sworn me in yet."

"I told you once, I'm telling you again, we're on the same side." He paused and looked her hard in the face. "Do you know something you're not telling?"

That Senior Class play, when she'd gotten the Worst Actor award hands-down, felt as if it had happened only yesterday. "About the pipe?" she said. "Of course not."

"About anything."

In the deathly silence of the small space, Hope felt faint.

If she accused Benton of some sort of collusion that was leaving him open to blackmail, she'd lose her chance at the vice presidency.

If she withheld her suspicions from Sam, he'd find out she lied to him.

If she kept quiet altogether, she couldn't live with herself.

Who should I be loyal to?

Why, to yourself.

What did the vice presidency matter if she couldn't live with herself?

What did anything matter if she couldn't have Sam.

The thought shook her to her very core. She was in love with him. How had that happened?

"Yes," she said. "I'm afraid there is something you ought to know."

HE WAS IN SHOCK, stunned by what she'd told him. True, he'd been waiting for Cap to come out in the open about his special interest in this case, but Hope had just managed to throw the man in the shark tank, directly into Sam's teeth.

"I did a very bad thing myself," Hope was saying to him, her words barely penetrating the fog in his mind, "by reading Benton's e-mail. I'll be in a lot of trouble for that. And I don't really have any proof, but I imagine it wouldn't be too hard to get. If Cap's getting big chunks of cash he has to be depositing it somewhere, so there be must a paper trail."

"It will destroy the firm." Sam's mouth was dry. "Could we get out of this closet?"

She led him into the living room and sat down on the sofa with her feet tucked up under her. Some instinct made him pull on his trousers before he glanced at the spot beside her, where he wanted to be, where he could touch her while they talked, but he took an armchair instead.

The firm would destroy him.

He was so close, so close. He'd paid his debts, he was breaking even, he was about to forge ahead to the comfortable spot he'd worked so hard, sacrificed so much to reach.

He felt like a lump of lead sitting there. What Hope had just told him had immobilized him, frozen his very soul inside his body. Because now he had to make a choice.

If he investigated Cap and found him culpable in the matter of a Palmer cover-up, the embarrassment to the firm would be infinite. And he'd be to blame for it, not Cap, but him. He'd lose everything.

It kept going around and around in his head, and Hope was waiting, waiting, he knew, for him to say, "This is an outrage. I'm blowing the whistle. To hell with the partnership. To hell with my future."

HOPE SAT QUIETLY, watching Sam, knowing she'd presented him with a virtually unsolvable problem and waiting for a chance to say, "I've fallen in love with you, Sam. We'll figure this out together, solve it together. It will be all right—as long as we're together."

She couldn't just blurt it out. Love was the furthest thing from his mind right now.

She knew enough about how the world worked to know the choices that faced him. She knew enough about Sam—she *thought* she knew enough about Sam—to count on him to make the right choice.

Suddenly unable to sit still another second, she went to the kitchen and started a pot of coffee. The answering-machine message light caught her eye again. She went over to it and punched the play button.

"Hi, hon!"

It was much too early in the morning, she felt far too tense, for Maybelle's special type of enthusiasm. She skipped on to the next message.

"Never figured you for a library user."

The voice, Cap's, jolted her. Behind her and across the room, she heard Sam's muttered oath. She wrapped her arms protectively across her chest and listened.

"I would never have noticed if you hadn't been wearing the same coat and scarf as the woman I saw at the housing project." He sounded amused. "My wife has that scarf."

Hope closed her eyes.

"Hey," Cap went on, "this is something we can handle between us. No problem, okay? You don't want to get your boss in trouble. Right? You don't want to cause any problems for—" he paused briefly "—our predatory friend."

Sam. He meant Sam. The Shark.

"He's probably there with you, come to think of it," Cap said, "but that's okay. We're all in this together. So let's meet tomorrow and talk over some alternatives. A little share of the take for each of you, maybe? At the library? Noonish? I'll see you—"

"The hell you will," Hope said, and crashed a finger down on the rewind button. She spun to find Sam standing just behind her. His face was gray.

"You think you're going to ruin him," Sam said. "In fact, he's going to ruin you."

"No, he's not. I won't let him."

"And me." His voice was so soft she could hardly hear him.

"No, he won't." She felt her face flushing hotly. "Nothing can ruin you except not being true to your own beliefs."

"People who announce that their bosses are paying blackmail money for good reason don't get to be vice president of Marketing." She hadn't expected him to be angry. "People who show that their law firms have covered up important evidence don't make partner!"

"So they go to another law firm! Another company! They go into business for themselves!" She was getting angry, too, and struggled for control. "I'm not suggesting we call a press conference here, Sam. I'm simply suggesting we find out the truth, I discuss the situation with Benton and you talk to Phil, and whatever happens we can go on with our lives knowing we did what was right."

We can go on with our lives. Together, because I—

"Right for whom."

"For the people at Magnolia Heights, for one thing."

She couldn't hold back the anger any longer. "They're the ones being punished."

He visibly calmed himself down. "Listen to me for a minute, Hope. We don't have to do anything rash. Okay, now, I'm thinking like a lawyer. This is what a good lawyer would do. I'll talk to Cap. Maybe we can manage to 'find new evidence'—work it so it looks like we've just learned whatever it is he already knows— before we try this case. We'll meet him at the library, see what he has to say."

"Absolutely not."

"You're not thinking clearly. You've gotten emotionally involved with the people at Magnolia Heights and you're not looking ahead."

"And you're not thinking about anybody but yourself."

Her words flew through the air like knives. He drew back.

"You don't know what the partnership means to me," he said quietly. "No way you could know."

"I don't even want to. Not anymore."

"If that's the way you want it."

"It is. And don't worry." The tears were threatening to break through and she bit her lip, trying to hold them back. "I won't do anything that will threaten your partnership. But I will do what I think is right for me, with or without you."

There was nothing in his face to show whether he cared or not. Wordlessly he pulled on the rest of his clothes, shouldered his briefcase and left.

She knew she would never see him again, and she could hardly bear it.

FIRST HOPE was dreaming, then she was having one of those half-asleep, half-awake dreams, and then, fully awake, she realized her eyes were hot with unshed tears.

Her subconscious had done the work for her while she slept, conjuring up a dream about Sam, about a life with him, and in those half-awake moments had filtered the dream into her consciousness. She knew she wanted all those things most people want—affection, passion and love, husband, children and a home—and furthermore that she could have them without giving up her career.

She just couldn't have them with Sam.

It would never have worked out anyway. She wouldn't be happy as a housewife and Sam wouldn't be happy as a househusband. They might have remembered the children's names, but their birthdays would be out of the question. Well, no, they would have recorded them in their Palm Pilots.

The tears spilled over. *Forget it.* The question of possibly working things out was moot. Their relationship had changed the moment she'd realized he cared more about his partnership than about doing what was right.

She wiped her eyes. No matter how depressed she was, she had work to do. She had one day, one single day, to turn her life around. She'd wear her scarlet suit. It might not help, but it couldn't hurt.

12

First Hope did her homework, going back to the Magnolia Heights files, looking up cost estimates, reading the final report in which Palmer had decided that submitting the lowest possible bid, meaning they'd make a slender profit on the job, would pay off in good public relations.

Although she didn't have access to their documents, it was clear that Stockwell Plumbing Contractors had made a similar decision along the way. There were communications urging efficient delivery of materials to cut costs, communications about coordination and cooperation between Palmer and Stockwell.

At the last possible minute, Hope gave up on sharpening her brains and went to work on her beauty.

Before she left the apartment in her scarlet suit, looking, she hoped, neither like a human tomato nor Santa Claus with swollen eyes, she watered the plants and left a message for the cleaning service that did its anonymous magic twice a week. Realizing she might not be home for a while, she gazed again at the changes Maybelle had made, the rounded lines of the tables, the fluffy rugs and covers, the terrycloth ottomans she'd put in the bathrooms. She'd even taken the edge off the galley-like kitchen with a charming wallpaper, shelf liners, an antique cookie jar.

Maybelle had done what she'd said she'd do. She'd taken away the sharp edges.

Hope saw that the same thing was happening to her. She was losing her sharp edges.

She needed them for one more day. Because today she was getting straight to the point.

She started in Slidell's cave. Today his hair was yellow—not blond, chrome yellow—and it went straight up on top, then curved over to create an interesting cockscomb effect. He looked like a Polish chicken she'd admired at a small-town State Fair their family had visited long ago.

But Slidell was no chicken. "You gave me access to Mr. Quayle's e-mail on that loaner," she said without preamble.

"I thought you'd never notice," Slidell said.

"Why? Why me?"

"I counted on you accidentally opening a message or two, figuring out something was going on and doing something about it. Everything goes through here," he said abruptly. "We know everybody's secrets. They assume we don't care enough about anything but bytes and RAM to notice what the words actually say. Well, we notice, but we keep our mouths shut."

"Until now."

"We're still keeping our mouths shut."

"You want me to talk to Benton."

"I know you'll do the right thing."

Hope was embarrassed to feel tears in her eyes. "I don't know what made you think you could trust me," she said haltingly, "but I feel—honored." It was the best word she could think of. "Magnolia Heights is your home, isn't it."

"No. My mother's. You went there."

She nodded.

"You saw what it was like."

She nodded again. A leaden feeling came over her. "So there *is* something wrong with the pipe."

"Ask Mr. Quayle."

She'd have to. Didn't want to, wasn't looking forward to it, but she had to live up to Slidell's opinion of her.

"Benton," she said a few minutes later, poking her head through the doorway, "can you give me a minute?"

"Sure." He looked as if he'd rather give her a kick in the rear end.

She stepped in, closed the door behind her and sat down opposite him.

"You're looking festive today," he said.

"I'm not feeling festive," she said, "and I suspect you aren't, either."

"Oh, every company has its legal battles, its little setbacks," Benton said, gesturing vaguely. "We'll get through it."

"Benton," she said gently, "I think there *is* something wrong with Number 12867. You know it, at least one person at Stockwell Plumbing knows it. Cap Waldstrum discovered it and he's blackmailing both of you."

Frightened, suddenly, by what she might have done, Hope watched the red flush climb Benton's face, watched his features harden. But his eyes told her he was stunned, confused. He looked like a hunted animal.

"It's you," he said. "You're the one who infiltrated my private communications. You. The last person I would ever have suspected."

"That part was an accident," Hope said, trusting her spine to hold her together a little longer. "But Benton, when I realized what was happening, I couldn't let it go on." She gazed at him. "You don't really want it to go on like this, do you?"

She saw the man she looked up to, the man she respected and admired, fall to pieces in front of her. "It was a die," he said. "The die we used for the first run of the nineties, the ninety degree angle joints," he added unnecessarily. He sounded like a bad recording, wooden and scratchy. "It got damaged somehow in the installation. They changed it as soon as they tested samples out of the first run, but there we were with a whole run that wasn't quite right."

"But the low bid meant the company couldn't afford to throw it away and start over."

"The low bid and the commitment to Stockwell to deliver on time."

"You told Stockwell the truth, didn't you."

"Yes. Just one person. Between us, we decided the joints couldn't do that much damage and it would be unlikely anyone would ever find them since they'd be installed randomly all over the project. They were such a small part of the whole plumbing system."

"Then Cap did some very thorough research when he was working on the settlement."

Benton's face darkened. "Found out the truth and decided to use it for personal profit."

"Surely he doesn't need the money," Hope whispered, remembering Cap's lavish life.

"Are you kidding?" Benton said tiredly. "He was broke, leveraged to the hilt and didn't have the guts to tell Muffy. Blackmail was a way out of the hole he was in."

"How much?" Hope asked.

The sum staggered her.

"You can't let him do this to you," she insisted.

Benton got up to pace back and forth behind his desk. "My responsibility is to the shareholders of this company." He darted a sharp glance at her. "You have a choice. I don't. You've got the vice presidency, Hope. You can take it, keep quiet, and life will go on."

"What about the people in Magnolia Heights? What about their lives?"

"They'll haunt me forever." He rested his hands on his desk and bowed his head. "But I can't betray the company."

Benton wasn't an evil person. He'd gotten stuck in the middle of his priorities—Palmer and his own sense of what was right. Who was she to say if he'd made the right choice or the wrong one?

Maybe she ought to show Sam the same generosity of spirit. But this was different. She wasn't thinking of sharing her life with Benton. She had her own choice to make, and she'd made it the night before.

"I'll submit my resignation at once, Benton," she said. "You'll have my letter by noon."

He only nodded.

She had one thing left to do. She called her friend Sandi to tell her how sorry she was that she couldn't make it to the party tonight after all.

SAM SAT at his gleaming rosewood desk contemplating the project that lay before him. It consisted of a wooden tongue-depressor-type coffee stirrer balanced on the edge of the desk. His goal was to flip a penny off the end of the coffee stirrer directly into a paper cup which still had a couple of inches of coffee in it.

What he had right now was a few pennies down under the surface of the cold coffee and a whole lot of pennies scattered all over the floor. He'd run out of pennies, in fact, and was moving on to dimes.

What he needed was an instrument more flexible than the coffee stirrer.

What he needed—was to take back everything that had happened the night before. What he needed was Hope.

The coffee he'd bought at a street stand and brought with him to the office wasn't as good as the coffee Hope made, the coffee she'd been making when she sent him out of her life.

But that wasn't why he needed her.

He needed her strength. He needed her strength the way his dad had needed his mom's strength. It was all starting to come clear to him. What happened to their family hadn't been his father's fault. Or the banker's fault or God's fault for holding back on the rain. It had just happened. It had happened to lots of people. And his mother had understood that and had stood behind the man she loved, worked with him, held him up, kept him going.

Just the way Hope would have done if he'd had the courage to imagine giving up one goal and setting out toward another one. The courage to start over.

He was in love with her and realizing it just in time to lose her. Now his life was—Hope-less.

It was too late to make her love him. But it wasn't too late to stop hating himself.

Instead of meeting Cap at the library, he made a swift trip to the Palmer plant in New Jersey and when he got back, did some rapid nosing around in things that were none of his business. As the result of his hard work, he was right there at the bank, behind Cap at the teller's window with a long line of people yelling at him to wait his turn, when Cap made a huge deposit in cash to an account under a different name.

It didn't take him long to get the story out of Cap. Just as he'd told Hope he would, he made a deal with Cap, but it wasn't quite the deal he'd told Hope he intended to make.

Each of the thousand times Hope had popped into his mind he'd felt exhausted, depressed by the knowledge that what he was doing wasn't going to bring her back. He was doing it for himself. Sam checked his watch. The partners would hold their annual meeting at six. He'd given Cap enough time to do what he'd promised to do. He squared his shoulders and went in to talk to Phil.

"This is terrible news, terrible," Phil said. He was pale with concern. "My responsibility is to the firm. I must protect its reputation at all costs."

"I know, sir." Sam stood up and shoved his hands in his pockets. "For that reason there are some things I'm not telling you. If I did, you'd have to take actions that would be even more embarrassing. The firm itself is not at fault."

There was no need to tell Phil about Cap. If Cap had kept his side of their deal, he'd resigned earlier in the day. He'd get another job. He would level with Muffy about their real financial situation. Muffy was a trooper. They'd sell the house, change lifestyles, tell their friends Cap had made a choice to leave the rat race and do something more meaningful. Together they'd make it.

For a minute Sam almost felt jealous of the man. His

own lonely road was going to be so much harder to travel.

"...have to handle this in a way that keeps the firm's reputation clean," Phil was saying.

Sam sat down heavily. This was the hard part. "As you said, sir, that's your responsibility. Mine is somewhat different."

Phil looked even more distressed. "But Sam, the partnership, your future..."

"Doesn't mean much to those folks at Magnolia Heights."

"No, I guess it doesn't." Phil sighed and closed his eyes. "Charlene is going to be deeply disappointed." He took a minute to reflect upon Charlene's disappointment, then turned a steady gaze on Sam.

"You're a good man, Sam Sharkey," he said. "Do what you have to do. I'll support you to the extent that I can."

"Thank you, Phil. The first thing I have to do is resign. Whatever I do, I'll be doing it independently."

"I was afraid that's what you were about to say." Phil's eyes sparked briefly. "That's two of you in one day. Seems Cap's leaving us."

"Is that so," Sam said.

"Says he feels a higher calling. Wants to do good for his fellow man. What's with you guys? Christmas getting to you?"

"You never know everything about a person, do you, Phil?" Sam said, getting up to leave.

"Not about some of them," Phil said.

Something in his voice made Sam turn back for one last look at him. He saw that Phil was smiling. It wasn't a happy smile, but it was an admiring one.

It was nearly six when he got back to his office. He

found the coffee cup gone and the pennies washed and gathered up from the floor and lying in a neat pile in a heavy glass ashtray on a newly gleaming desk. There were some things he'd miss about this job. Summoning up all the courage he had left, he gritted his teeth and called Hope.

"This is Hope Sumner," said Hope's familiar, smooth and professional voice. "I am not able to take your call. If this is an emergency, please dial zero now."

Zero wasn't going to be much help to him, so he dialed her at home. "You've reached 212-555-1313." Her voice sounded depressed now. It must be a new message. His heart was already thudding violently when he heard, "I'll be out of the city until the Sunday after Christmas. Please leave your name and number..."

He hung up. She'd gone home early. He supposed he could call every Sumner in Chicago until he found her...

Or not.

He could go home early himself, rent a car at the airport and pop in on the folks, surprise the socks off them.

Or not.

For a long time he just sat there, too sad to take any action at all.

MAGGIE AND HANK SUMNER were delighted to see Hope arrive late Friday night instead of Saturday. Hank took her bag up to her old room, and Maggie led her into the kitchen. "You must have a piece of my snowball cake," she insisted.

"No, thanks, Mom," Hope said. "You know how I love your coconut cake, but I ate so much for dinner..."

"You ate on the plane," Hank said, joining them at the kitchen table. "That's not dinner."

Hope looked at her parents fondly. They were in their sixties now, but in Hope's eyes her mother just got more beautiful every year, her blond hair silvering gracefully, her figure still trim and her smile—it would never change, never lose its warmth and hint of feistiness.

If she hadn't been feisty, she'd never have made it through their childhoods.

Hank still taught history courses at the University of Chicago, swearing he'd never retire. They still lived in Oak Lawn where the girls had grown up, in the same Craftsman-style, homey, comfortably shabby house.

"It's so good to be here," she said simply. She managed a smile. "Okay, cut me a chunk of that cake and I'll take it up to bed with me."

Hope slept late on Saturday, then helped her mother make batch after batch of cookies. "I'll never forget that day," Maggie said nostalgically as she dripped frosting onto the angel cutout cookies, "that day you three girls showed up at the door."

Hope would never forget that day, either. Out of sheer determination and an organizational ability she must have been born with—she'd only been six at the time—she'd gotten the three of them away from their mother's family and brought them here, to Maggie and Hank, which had been their mother's wish.

"I especially remember the look on your face," Maggie said. "Determined, stubborn... I didn't know until I put my arms around you and felt you shaking that you were scared to death."

"I don't think I started shaking until you gave me that hug," Hope said. "I suddenly realized that maybe we were home free, that maybe somebody else could take over for a while. If I'd let down my guard for even a second in front of Faith and Charity, we wouldn't have made it here."

"You were always their leader," Maggie said. "Still are." She arched an eyebrow. "I even think Faith and Charity are waiting for you to fall in love first, test the waters before they jump, so to speak."

Hope's eyes widened. "Then you're never going to have any grandchildren," she said wildly, "because I'm never...I'm never..."

"Hope, baby, what is this?"

When Maggie laid a hand on Hope's shoulder and looked at her so sympathetically, Hope sat down with a thud at the kitchen table and cried all over the yellow-frosted stars.

But she still couldn't talk about it.

FAITH'S PLANE was arriving late that afternoon. Charity, who had a cottage in the country north of Chicago, picked her up at the airport, so they arrived together in a flurry of laughter, hugs, kisses and untidy parcels of gifts. Their first question after the hugging was over was about Sam.

"It didn't work out," Hope said, smiling a smile she'd practiced in the mirror. "Nice while it lasted, though."

They would never know how nice it had been, nice, naughty, hot and fulfilling. What it was now was over. No, it had not worked out. That was the truth.

"I'm getting the cat as soon as I get back to New York," she told them as they sat around the Christmas tree sipping coffee after one of Maggie's wonderful pot roast dinners.

Her sisters were treating her with unusual delicacy. They might be the world's worst teases, but not when they knew she was unhappy. "What kind?" Charity said brightly.

"I still haven't decided. All suggestions appreciated."

A lively discussion ensued. Conversations at the Sumner house always seemed to turn lively, even conversations about cats.

"The long-haired ones are gorgeous, but they shed all over the place," Charity warned her. Charity had a houseful of pets, strays she'd brought home.

"Are you sure you aren't allergic to cats?" Maggie asked her.

"No."

"Oh, well," Faith said, "if you turn out to be they have shots for it, don't they?"

"That's a typical reaction from you," Charity said. "Keep the cat, take a shot."

"You'd do the same thing," Faith countered.

"Yes, I guess I would," Charity admitted.

"Siamese, I understand," Hank said in his slow, thoughtful way, "are less apt to cause an allergic reaction than some of the other breeds."

"White cats with blue eyes are usually deaf," Charity said.

"I wasn't planning to talk to it much," Hope said. "Or at least I wasn't thinking about any deep, meaningful conversations."

"In cats, the mixed breeds are often preferable." This was Hank again, quoting, undoubtedly, something he'd read.

"I bought a book," Hope said. "But what I'll probably do is go to an animal shelter and take home the cat that speaks to me."

"That might be the best thing to do," Maggie said. "Rely on your own best judgment."

"Let us know, so we can send presents," Charity said.

"I hardly think presents are called for in this..."

Hope had suddenly gotten distracted by the television set they hadn't bothered to turn off in the kitchen. The words she'd heard were "Magnolia Heights." She got up and moved toward the sound.

On the screen she saw a scene of utter chaos as police, firefighters and television crews fought for space on the lawns of Magnolia Heights. Glaring lights showed that they weren't exactly lawns any more. They were more like lakes. Hope gasped, already knowing what she was about to hear.

"...a disaster on a major scale," a frozen-looking reporter said. "Magnolia Heights has been engaged in a legal battle for several months involving the plumbing leaks that have plagued the project from the beginning. What happened tonight will probably lead to the restitution the parties involved have so far refused to agree to. Major breakage occurred in Building B, flooding the grounds..."

"Oh, no," Hope whispered, thinking of Mrs. Hotchkiss and her teething baby, of Slidell's mother, Mrs. Hchiridski.

She found that her family had gathered behind her. Charity said, "Isn't this the project..."

"Yes," Hope said, and then, "Sam!"

His face, grim, haggard and unshaven, filled the

screen as reporters shouted, "Mr. Sharkey! May I ask you..."

"Is that Sam Sharkey?" Faith breathed. "Oh, Lord, Hope, he's gor..."

"Sh-h-h," Charity said fiercely.

"Mr. Sharkey, is it true you were assigned to argue the Palmer Pipe case in court?"

"No comment."

"Mr. Sharkey!" The shout came from the back of the mob of reporters and cameramen. "Is it true you resigned your position at Brinkley Meyers today?"

"Resigned," Hope breathed. "Oh, Sam..."

"No comment."

"Does your resignation have anything to do with new evidence..."

Hope whirled, filled with a wild need for action. "I have to go back," she said abruptly.

"Oh, honey, you can't," her mother pleaded with her. "It's Christmas. The problem's not going to go away. It will still be waiting for you when you get back."

"Mom," Faith said gently, "you know how Hope feels about her job. She can't help feeling responsible."

"It's not my job," Hope said distinctly.

The news story faded into the background.

"I quit my job. I'm going back to help Sam."

As she raced out of the kitchen to call the airline, she heard Charity say, "Oh. My. Gosh," to an otherwise silent room.

13

SAM WAS SITTING in a chair in front of the television set in a dead sleep of total physical and emotional exhaustion when the pipes broke. The words that had gripped Hope's attention woke him up. "Magnolia Heights."

He was already hopping into the first clothes that fell out of the cluttered closet and into his hands by the time the reporter got to the words "...at the present temperature of seven degrees Fahrenheit, the water is rapidly forming a sheet of ice approximately three to four inches thick around the three buildings, creating hazardous conditions for..."

In the next few minutes he cursed everything from his shoelaces to his zipper to the concept of plumbing, reviving colorful expletives he hadn't used since his high school days. He was dressed by the time he heard, "At present, there is no water supply to Building B. Residents of the other two buildings have offered shelter to..."

And last, "...won't find much Christmas spirit at Magnolia Heights this year as residents struggle to..."

On his way out the door, he remembered he was flying, that he had once thought he would be flying, to Nebraska tomorrow. He had to call his folks.

His father answered. "Dad, I can't come home tomorrow. I've got a crisis here."

He listened for a minute to the protests, then heard his mother take over the phone. "You go right ahead and take care of that problem at Magnolia Heights," she said. "We've been hearing about those poor people on the news. We'll let the grandkids have their Christmas. The grown-ups will wait until you get here."

"Thanks, Mom." Listening to her, he felt like a kid himself again. "But you don't have to wait."

"I know, but we will. Doesn't matter whether we have Christmas on the twenty-fifth. All that matters is that..."

"...we'll be with each other," Sam said softly. It had taken him this long to find out that his mother was right.

There was no time now to think about his family and how grateful he was to have them. He ran down to Houston Street, figuring that was his best chance for a cab at this hour. The impact of the disaster kept beating at him—no water, sheet of ice, residents bunking in with strangers—all the long distance north to Magnolia Heights. Too little too late. No one could ever make it right, but he was damned sure going to give it a try.

HOPE ARRIVED in New York at four in the morning, sleepless and wired on airline coffee. While she packed, she'd assigned Charity to the computer and Faith to the phone. Between them they'd located a Samuel Sharkey on Avenue B, in an area of New York which was just now beginning to be occupied by young professional people. She was going straight to his apartment. He had to let her in. He had to talk to her. She'd thought of one thing, one small thing that, while it wouldn't solve anything, might at least make everyone feel better. It was so trivial she was almost embarrassed to mention it, but at least it was something.

The taxi pulled up to a four-story town house. It had clearly not felt the touch of gentrification. Hope paid the driver and went up the front stoop to find a call box like the one outside Building B at Magnolia Heights. She found "Sharkey, Sam" in 4R and pushed the buzzer.

There was no answer. But of course he'd be asleep. So she'd wake him up. Grimly she buzzed again. And again.

At last she stood back from the call box and glared at it. If he was out, she'd wait for him. If he was in and not answering, she'd kill him when he came out.

She was beginning to feel the cold through her wool socks, through her snow boots and even through the down coat Charity had insisted on loaning her. She sat on the stoop and leaped up at once. It was like sitting on a glacier.

She began to pace the sidewalk, blowing on her fingertips. It was so dark. The streetlamps seemed dimmer than the ones outside her apartment building. She could see Christmas lights behind some of the nearby windows, but at this hour they seemed menacing rather than cheerful, glowing red like rats' eyes. She wished she hadn't thought about rats. She'd never felt so alone.

At once she wished she *were* alone. A derelict staggered out of the shadows, moving down the sidewalk toward her. Hope shrank back toward the stoop and the shelter of the doorway, but he'd seen her, he was going to speak to her.

She folded her hands under her chin in a prayerful pose. "God bless ye, merry gentlemen," she sang in a quavering voice, turning her face toward the upper windows of the town house, "let nothing you dismay, for Jesus Christ our Sa-a-vior was..."

"...bored on Chrishmash Day," sang the derelict, stumbling on down the sidewalk. "To shave us all from..."

Hope let out a whoosh of relief, forgiving him completely for being off-key, and resumed her pacing.

There had to be an all-night coffee shop somewhere close. This was New York, the city that never slept. But she couldn't leave her post. She couldn't miss her chance to see Sam when he came home—or kill him when he came out.

She stomped her feet against the pavement, hoping to warm them. They were already so numb with cold it didn't hurt a bit. So she stood a while, stomping, then paced a while, stomping, huddled in the down coat and colder than she'd ever been in her entire life.

Now and then she ran up the stoop and rang Sam's buzzer ten more times. It made a change in the routine. She had just finished doing it again when a police car cruised down the street and pulled up to the curb beside her.

"Time to go home, Lola," one of the officers called out, speaking to her through a window opened two inches.

She stepped over to the car. "I'm not Lola, I'm..."

"Sorry. This is Lola's block. Better not let her catch you here. Well, whoever you are, get yourself home."

"I can't," Hope said. "I'm waiting for someone."

"Sure, sure," he said. "That's what all you girls are doing. Waiting for someone. Come on, lady, go home before you freeze to death."

Even as thickheaded as she felt, his meaning finally became clear. "I'm not a prostitute," she said in an outraged tone. "I'm a friend of someone who lives in that building." She pointed.

"I said go home."

He'd been genial before. Now his voice had hardened. Hope began to grope with numb fingers in her handbag, looking for identification that would prove she was an honest, upright businesswoman. It startled her when the door of the patrol car flew open.

"Okay, that's it. Drop the purse and get in the car."

"What?"

"I said, get in the car." He grabbed her arm. "You won't go home peaceful-like, I have to take you in."

A taxi came by. Hope was thinking of flinging herself in front of it when it stopped and Sam stepped out of it, looked up, saw her and took on an expression of utter astonishment. "Hope?" he said.

"Well. Finally," she snarled at him. "*Where have you been*, you worthless excuse for a..."

The officer loosened his hold on her arm and she snatched it away angrily.

"This lady a friend of yours?"

Sam looked as if he'd love to deny it.

"Sam Sharkey," she said warningly.

"Yes," he said.

"Need any help with her?"

Sam hesitated again until Hope stamped her foot. "No."

"Okay, then. Sorry about the confusion." Genial again, the officer got back into the car and it moved off.

"What are you doing here?"

"I have to talk to you."

He looked helpless, his gaze going back and forth between her and his doorway. "Here?"

"Yes, here, you imbecile!" she shouted at him. "Take me inside at once or you'll have my frozen body to deal with!"

"Oh. Yes. Sorry." He hurried her into the building.

She hardly saw the grim, stained stairwell as they climbed three flights of stairs to a doorway at the rear of the building. She hardly noticed the stairs because Sam had picked her up and carried her two of the flights.

When he'd gotten the door open he laid her down carefully on a soft surface. He turned on the light and she saw that she was on his bed. He snuggled a comforter around her and went to a small stove in what seemed to be the kitchen part of the one-room apartment, where he put a kettle of water on to heat.

For a few minutes, Hope just lay there and shuddered. So this was how Sam lived. Saving his money, not spending on himself except where he had to, to keep up appearances. He'd said she wouldn't be able to understand how much the partnership mattered to him. Now she was beginning to, but it sounded as if he'd done the right thing anyway. Her heart filled with sudden joy, driving away the cold.

He turned away from the stove and came over to her, sat down on the edge of the bed, reached under the coverlet and took off her snow boots. She watched him with wide eyes as he began to massage her feet. The feeling began to come back into them—and into her heart.

"What were you doing outside at six o'clock in the morning? Auditioning for *The Little Match Girl*?"

His eyes were veiled, his expression inscrutable. She'd broken his heart. How wonderful. It meant he did care for her. Maybe he even loved her. But even if he didn't now, he would when she got through with him.

"Ask me what I was doing there at four," she said.

"What were you..."

"Not literally," she snapped. "I told you. I need to talk to you." His heart would mend. She'd see to it, night and day for the rest of her life.

"This is the twenty-first century. We have telephones."

"This was faster," she said.

She could see him trying to figure that one out. "You are aware of radio and television," he said. "You heard the news."

"There is no other news," she said. "If Jesus had been born last night Christianity wouldn't have had a chance."

He didn't even smile. "It's bad," he said. "I stayed up there until they got the building evacuated and started work on the water system. They're blowing heaters on the sidewalks, too, to cut down on the accidents." He gazed at her blankly for a moment. "You're in Chicago."

Had the man completely lost his swiftness of brain? "I was, but now I'm here. I have an idea." It wasn't the only reason, but the rest could come later.

He got up again, poured an inch of brandy into a glass and added boiling water to it. "Drink this," he said, "then hit me with your idea."

So she did.

"Hope," he said when she'd finished, "how can we do something like that in twenty-four hours?"

"Santa Claus," she reminded him, "does it in one night."

It was Christmas Eve and the atmosphere at Magnolia Heights was festive. Benton had been almost pathetically cooperative. Palmer Pipe had supplied the railings that surrounded the skating rink that had once been the front lawn of Building B at Magnolia Heights. The general contractor who'd built the buildings had put them up. Sprightly music came from loudspeakers as colorful skaters swooped around the ice in skates supplied by Stockwell Plumbing Contractors.

The City of New York Parks Department had brought out an enormous Christmas tree. Private donors had assembled a mountain of gifts. Vendors distributed free hot dogs, cocoa and cotton candy, courtesy of Brinkley Meyers. A clown on skates entertained the younger children with his antics.

Hope moved closer and stared at him. Could that be St. Paul the Perfect? The clown waved at her and made his mouth go way down at the corners. Ah, the perks that came with being the new vice president of Marketing at Palmer Pipe.

Television cameras formed a ring around the scene. In the late afternoon, they moved as if summoned by the Pied Piper to a spot at the edge of the rink. Palmer and Stockwell had called a press conference to announce that their companies would foot the cost of replumbing Magnolia Heights. "This was a grave, grave situation for these wonderful people to find themselves in," Benton said, shaking his jowls. "Whether the fault lies with us or elsewhere, we accept responsibility and we'll make it right."

"Oh, my goodness gracious, isn't that fine?" Maybelle said, scooting up to stand beside Hope.

Hope smiled at her. "Couldn't be finer."

"Well, yes it could." Maybelle frowned. "I just took a tour of that place," she said, pointing toward Building C, "and whoo-ee, hon, I want to tell you the way the *Ch'i* is flowin' in there it's no wonder some of them folks aren't gettin' on better than they are."

"Well, Maybelle," Hope said patiently, "some people just don't have a lot of money to spend on their homes."

"I'm not talkin' about spending any money," Maybelle scoffed. "You young folks, that's all you can think about. Money. I'm just talkin' about arranging the stuff you've already got, gettin' it in order. That's all I did for you, basically. You know what I'm gonna do?"

"Send me my bill?" Hope said faintly.

"I'm gonna give a bunch of feng shui seminars."

"Why, Maybelle, that's a wonderful idea. If you kept the cost low, like five dollars a session..."

"Oh, hon, I'm not going to charge," Maybelle said. She gazed dreamily into the distance. "Me, a teacher. Now that's one thing I've never been."

"It's clear you've never been an accountant, either," Hope said pointedly. "If you would just send me a—"

"—bill. Oh, yeah. I gotta get around to that one of these days. Well, have yourself a Merry Christmas," Maybelle said, and fluttered away.

The thing that had been about to burst out of Hope bubbled high inside her again and she looked around for Sam. He was nowhere to be found.

HOPE SAT on the floor and stared at the Christmas tree. There was still one gift under it, the gift she'd gotten Sam, a luxurious cashmere sweater exactly the color of his eyes.

It was a great gift. All she needed was Sam to give it to.

She leaned back against the nearest chair and closed her eyes. It would never have worked between Sam and her. In her mind's eye, she saw the nanny sitting with the children in front of the Christmas tree. Mommy and Daddy weren't up yet. They were very tired, because Mommy's pipes had broken and Daddy had had to put up a skating rink overnight.

"That," Hope said, opening her eyes, "is ridiculous."

Feeling the tears start up again, she reminded herself that she'd be just fine. She was flying back to Chicago tomorrow to finish her truncated Christmas visit, and when she got back to New York, healed and soothed by the love of her family, she would get a cat and a new job.

Not pipe. Something else. She'd outgrown pipe.

She would never outgrow the memories of Sam. Even now she could feel his fingertips against her skin, hear the deep chords of his voice, feel herself burning with need for him.

She snatched up the cat book and thumbed through it. When the telephone rang, she told herself not to get excited. Her parents would call tonight. That's who it probably—

"Hi."

"Sam?" His name trembled on her tongue.

"Is this a bad time?"

Yes, you idiot, it's a terrible time. I'm sitting here all by myself, crying, looking through a damned cat book, and wondering if I should go into retailing! Is that any way to spend Christmas Eve?

"No," she said more smoothly than she'd spoken before, "I'm just sitting here enjoying the Christmas tree."

"I have a little present for you. May I bring it by?"

As always, there were sounds in the background, some of them very strange indeed. "I suppose so," she said. "I have a little gift for you, too."

"I'll see you in about...a minute and a half," he said.

When she opened the door to him, she had to struggle not to leap at him with arms opened wide, begging him for forgiveness and an immediate hug. It would have been difficult for him to give her an immediate hug anyway, because he carried a pet crate in each hand and had a single, scratchy-looking red bow stuck in the pocket of his overcoat.

"What?" she said. "What is that? Are those?" There wasn't much doubt about what they were. Annoyed mewing sounds came from both crates.

"I'll show you," he said.

He opened one crate, and out stepped a kitten. She recognized it from the picture in the cat book, a long-haired Himalayan, pale, blue-eyed and breathtakingly beautiful.

"Oh, Sam, she's gorgeous," she said, getting down on the floor to run her hand through its fur.

"He," Sam said. "She's a he."

The kitten prissed disdainfully around Hope's knees, then sniffed her hand.

"Hold on," Sam said, and opened the second crate. A bolt of yellow flew out, skidded to a stop, looked straight up at Hope and all but said, "About time!" before it jumped on her lap, dug all ten tiny claws through her velvet leggings and then climbed her silk shirt.

Her former silk shirt. After a yelp of pain, she laughed out loud. "He?" she said.

"She."

"Oh." She was thin, even scrawny, a yellow-striped tiger kitten with yellow-green eyes that narrowed as she assessed the room and imagined its possibilities.

"I love them," Hope said fervently. "Thank..."

"You have to pick one. I only brought one bow." He took the bow out of his pocket and flourished it at her.

Dismayed, she stared at him. "Pick one? How can I pick one? Just think how the other one would feel."

His dark blue eyes swam across her face, making her dizzy with their intensity. "It will feel fine. Pick one."

"Could we talk for a minute while I think?"

"No. First judgments are usually the best. Pick."

The Himalayan jumped onto the sofa and curled himself into a perfectly round ball, gently purring. An alarming sound came from the bedroom, where the tiger kitten had apparently gone exploring.

"I can't."

"I'll give you the comparative data. The Himalayan's a purebred. He's about a fifteen-hundred-dollar cat, as fine a specimen as you could hope for."

"Oh, Sam, you can't afford..."

"Hush. It's Christmas. The tiger came from Animal Rescue, runt of the litter, abandoned by the mother. Five bucks, shots included." Still he gazed at her.

Hope took a deep breath. She gazed at the peaceful sight of the Himalayan asleep on her sofa. He matched it. You could sit down on a cat like that and never know it until it was too late.

She followed the ominous sounds into her bedroom. The tiger had knocked the new set of candles off the dresser and was batting one of them across the floor with her paw, apparently thrilled that it rolled. When she saw Hope, she paused in her game, tilted her head up and looked Hope straight in the eyes.

She smiled. "Yes," she said softly. She bent down, petted the kitten and felt her little back arch up under the caress. Hope wiped away a tear and picked her up. The kitten relaxed at once in her arms. Hope rocked her for a moment, then went back to Sam.

He was still waiting in the living room, his eyes

watchful. "We've decided to be roomies," she said, cuddling the kitten.

"Thank God!" Sam said, flinging himself down in an armchair in a position of collapsed relief. "The Himalayan belongs to the department secretary—my former department secretary," he amended himself. "She's downstairs in the lobby even as we speak, on pins and needles waiting for me to bring back her fifteen-hundred-dollar baby."

Hope put the kitten down gently, then flung herself on him. "Oh, Sam, Sam, you are a devil, an absolute devil." She felt herself starting to sob, or maybe she was laughing, or maybe it was something in between, as she pounded at his shoulders. "Why did you do that? What if I'd chosen the Himalayan? What would you have done?"

His body grew very still, although his hands caressed her back. "I trusted you," he said, "to pick the cat with character."

She stilled, too, pulled away from him a little. "Can you ever forgive me for not trusting you?"

"I have to. For a minute there I forgot who I really was. I didn't deserve your trust." He pulled her back down to him, stretching her out over the length of his body. "Do you trust me now? Remember, I'm unemployed. Do you trust me to get another job, be a responsible member of society?"

"You mean earn part of the family income?" Hope said, stroking kisses across his throat, wishing she could devour him in one wonderful gulp. "I'm unemployed, too," she said. "It's a great window of opportunity for having a baby."

He made a low, muffled sound as he gripped her even more tightly. "We'll be okay, won't we, as long as..."

"...as long as we have each..." Hope said, moving her body against his, seeking his heat, his hardness, wanting him so badly she didn't think she could finish another sentence until she'd had all of him she could steal.

His mouth closed down on hers, gently at first but quickly seizing her with all the passion she could feel inside him. She wrenched at the buttons of his shirt, then her blouse, wanting more of him against herself, wanting to feel the crisp hair on his chest brushing her breasts.

"Oh, God, Carol," he muttered.

She stiffened, suddenly feeling faint, dizzy and sick at heart. She drew back from him. "You called me by another woman's name." Her lips could barely form the words.

"Carol. The secretary," he groaned. "Downstairs in the lobby. Waiting for her cat. I forgot all about her."

Hope rolled off him. "For heaven's sake, Sam. Pull yourself together. Where'd the kittens go?"

Sam was buttoning rapidly. "I don't know. Find the Himalayan." He looked down at himself. "Oh, my God, I'll have to wear my overcoat. Do I have lipstick anywhere that shows?" He ran nervous fingers through his tousled hair.

She found the Himalayan in the office alcove. Curled up on her desk like that, he looked a lot like a mouse pad. Quickly popping him back in his crate, she handed the crate to Sam. "And hurry," she said.

She followed him all the way to the door, hardly able to let him go even for a minute. As she turned back into the room, the Christmas tree swayed. Hope swayed with it, then directed her gaze to the top. The tiger kitten was there, engaged in a battle to the death with the pipe star.

"You're going to fit in just fine around here," she told the kitten as she dug its claws out of the Styrofoam ball.

And so would Sam.

HOPE NAMED *the kitten Ch'i.*

They had Christmas with Sam's family first, then with Hope's. Ch'i went with them.

In February, Hope and Sam formed their own consulting firm.

They were married in March, thinking that if working together hadn't driven them to a knock-down-drag-out fight yet, the marriage had a fair chance of lasting.

Susannah Sumner-Sharkey was born the following Christmas Day after a short, efficient labor. She has a nursery in their office suite, and comes to work with them every day.

So does Ch'i. They have no mice. They have, however, had to replace the curtains twice.

Maybelle does all their decorating.

She still hasn't sent Hope a bill.

Two city gals are about to turn life upside
down for two Wyoming ranchers in

Cowboy Country

Two full-length novels of true
Western lovin' from favorite authors

JUDITH BOWEN
RENEE ROSZEL

Available in January 2002 at your favorite retail outlet.

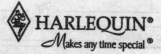

HARLEQUIN®
Makes any time special ®

BR2CC

CALL THE ONES YOU LOVE OVER THE HOLIDAYS!

Save $25 off future book purchases when you buy any four Harlequin® or Silhouette® books in October, November and December 2001,

PLUS

receive a phone card good for 15 minutes of long-distance calls to anyone you want in North America!

WHAT AN INCREDIBLE DEAL!

Just fill out this form and attach 4 proofs of purchase (cash register receipts) from October, November and December 2001 books, and Harlequin Books will send you a coupon booklet worth a total savings of $25 off future purchases of Harlequin® and Silhouette® books, AND a 15-minute phone card to call the ones you love, anywhere in North America.

Please send this form, along with your cash register receipts as proofs of purchase, to:
In the USA: Harlequin Books, P.O. Box 9057, Buffalo, NY 14269-9057
In Canada: Harlequin Books, P.O. Box 622, Fort Erie, Ontario L2A 5X3
Cash register receipts must be dated no later than December 31, 2001.
Limit of 1 coupon booklet and phone card per household.
Please allow 4-6 weeks for delivery.

I accept your offer! Enclosed are 4 proofs of purchase. Please send me my coupon booklet and a 15-minute phone card:

Name: _____

Address: _____ City: _____

State/Prov.: _____ Zip/Postal Code: _____

Account Number (if available): _____

097 KJB DAG
PHQ40

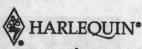

HARLEQUIN®

makes any time special—online...

eHARLEQUIN.com

your romantic life

—Romance 101—
♥ Guides to romance, dating and flirting.

—Dr. Romance —
♥ Get romance advice and tips from our expert, Dr. Romance.

—Recipes for Romance —
♥ How to plan romantic meals for you and your sweetie.

—Daily Love Dose—
♥ Tips on how to keep the romance alive every day.

—Tales from the Heart—
♥ Discuss romantic dilemmas with other members in our Tales from the Heart message board.

Look to the stars
for love and romance
with bestselling authors

JUDITH ARNOLD
KATE HOFFMANN
and GINA WILKINS

in

WRITTEN
IN THE
STARS

Experience the joy of
three women who dare to
make their wishes for love
and happiness come true in
this *brand-new* collection
from Harlequin!

Available in December 2001
at your favorite retail outlet.

HARLEQUIN®
Makes any time special ®

ADDED BONUS:
As a special gift to our readers, a 30-page 2002
Love Guide will be included in this collection!

Visit us at www.eHarlequin.com   PHWS

*Together for the first time
in one Collector's Edition!*

New York Times bestselling authors

Barbara
Delinsky

Catherine
Coulter

Linda
Howard

Forever
Yours

**A special trade-size volume containing three
complete novels that showcase the passion,
imagination and stunning power that these
talented authors are famous for.**

Coming to your favorite retail outlet in December 2001.

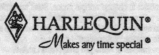

If you enjoyed what you just read,
then we've got an offer you can't resist!

Take 2 bestselling love stories FREE!

Plus get a FREE surprise gift!